SLEIGH RIDE WITH THE COWBOY

A HUCKLEBERRY FALLS HOLIDAY ROMANCE

JEN PETERS

BLUE LILY BOOKS

To Blaik, my handsome, not-quite-cowboy sweetheart

SLEIGH RIDE WITH THE COWBOY

1

W es Colton felt like he'd taken a wrong turn and landed in a whole different state. Or country.

His truck still hummed along the plowed highway, heaps of grungy snow lining the asphalt, but the air left his lungs, and his tired body sagged.

"This doesn't look like the Huckleberry Falls I remember," he told Kuda, the silver Husky beside him. The dog lifted his head slightly then dropped it again. He was tired, too.

Wes had hoped for a bit of a homecoming feeling when he passed the *Welcome to Huckleberry Falls* sign, but there was only the slightest twinge of familiarity.

Sure, Wes knew the town had been changing. The powers that be had started revamping Huckleberry Falls' image more than a decade ago, before he left high school. He knew the dilapidated strip mall just out of town had been re-faced to match the Swiss village feel of Main Street. There were new stores, and some empty lots on the way in now sported high-end boutiques. They'd been rebranding the whole town,

1

spotlighting the skiing, the outdoor sports, and the holidays. But…

Wow. Just wow.

Tiny white lights covered every post, every porch, every window. Pine trees in the Town Square blazed red, green, and gold, towered over by a magnificently decorated tree in the center. He could turn his headlights off and not have any problems driving.

Even Kuda was sitting up and looking out the window now.

And then there were the people. Crowds on the sidewalks, crowds in the Square, crowds in and out of the stores. And enough traffic that it took him two light cycles to get through the intersections.

Nine years was a long time, though, and his only visits back had centered around his grandmother, not the holidays or the skiing. He'd spent pretty much all of his time at her home, her doctor's office, and a trip or two to the grocery store, without paying much attention to the differences in town. It wasn't like he was going to shop at the fancy new stores, after all.

Wes's stomach rumbled loudly, reminding him that he hadn't eaten anything but gas station snacks since breakfast in Colorado Springs. Kuda nosed him and let out a small whine.

"I know, boy. Past time we eat something, isn't it?" He needed something more substantial than a pastry from Torta al Cioccolato, but when he looked beyond the twinkling lights for his favorite Italian diner, he saw it had been replaced by a fancy restaurant called Miraval. What was it with foreign names? Wes glanced ruefully at his jeans and wrinkled shirt; even if he had the inclination to try a place like that, he wasn't fit to be seen inside there.

With another sigh, he pulled into the McDonald's

parking lot a few blocks on. He worked through the soreness as his muscles stretched and complained on the way to the entrance. His well-worn cowboy boots slid once on the thin, slick layer of snow, but he kept his balance. Good thing, too —there were too many people around to make a fool of himself.

ONE BIG MAC (plus one for Kuda), one large fries and a shake later, Wes felt like he could face the outside world again. And if he could do that, he could face Grandma's empty house. It shouldn't be any different than when she'd been in the nursing home, but the thought that she wouldn't ever be coming back... Grief washed over him once more for this loving woman who had basically raised him through his teenage years. His world was emptier, knowing she wasn't there rooting for him anymore. But he could do this one last thing for her.

He pulled Old Faithful, his F-350 pickup, into the driveway, despite the foot of accumulated snow on it. Tomorrow would be full of shoveling, obviously. Kuda jumped down eagerly and bounded through the snow.

"Stay close, boy." He shone his phone flashlight on the door and had just inserted the key when he heard a voice.

"Wes Colton, is that you?"

Wes turned. "Yes, Mrs. McCarthy, it's me."

The older woman approached carefully, keeping her knee-high boots in his footsteps. She pulled her sheepskin coat close around her. "We sure do miss your grandma. I can't believe it's been almost a year."

Wes turned the key in the lock. "I know. I'm sorry I couldn't stay long after the funeral."

"That's all right, honey." Mrs. McCarthy patted his arm.

"You have all that work on that ranch, don't you? I'm just glad you're here now. Don't like having an empty house next door. And who's this handsome fellow?"

"His name's Kuda. Got him a few years ago." Kuda sniffed her fingers as Wes pushed the door open. "Come on in out of the wind, Mrs. M." Although it was almost as cold inside as it was out. He flicked the light switch, but nothing happened. He flicked it again.

"No, Wes, don't you remember they turned off the water and electricity? Winterized the house and all." She stepped in after him, her face half shadowed in the flashlight glow.

Wes closed the door, then leaned his head against it. He'd pushed all day to get here in time to settle for the night. His body cried out for the comfort of his teenage bed, even without Grandma here to welcome him. There was no way he and Kuda could stay here tonight.

"No, there isn't," Mrs. McCarthy agreed.

Great. Now he was thinking out loud. "I guess I'll get a hotel room."

Mrs. McCarthy shook her head. "It's the Festival of Trees weekend, plus this snow has pulled in a boatload of skiiers. Most of the hotel rooms are spoken for. And I've got every bed plus the couch full of grandkids right now, or I'd invite you over. But maybe…"

Wes looked at her with weary hope.

"Let me call Lizbeth Williams. They've got that Bed & Breakfast just south of town." She held her hand up as Wes started to interrupt. "I know they're full up, but I also know she's got a tiny box room with a twin bed that she keeps for emergencies. Let's see if it's got a body in it already."

Five minutes later, Wes had an invitation to stay at the B&B that even included Kuda. One night only, but hopefully he could get the electricity and water on tomorrow.

"Thanks, Mrs. M. I'm not sure what we would have done if you hadn't come over." He locked the front door and walked her back to her house.

"You tell Mac at the town offices to do what it takes to get power on tomorrow. And if it really is impossible, I'll shove a kid onto the floor for you."

Wes gave her a long hug and trudged back to his truck where Kuda was flipping snow with his nose. No Grandma, no house to stay in, no homey feel to the town. Kuda was happy, but Wes didn't care if the bed in the little room was a foot too short for his six-foot frame; it couldn't come soon enough.

"THANKS, MRS. WILLIAMS," Wes said the next morning, backpack slung over his shoulder, the Husky by his side. "You honestly don't know how much this meant to me last night."

"I understand," Mrs. Williams smiled. "That's why we keep that room instead of using it for storage. You tell Mrs. McCarthy I'll let her take me to lunch sometime."

"I will, ma'am, and thanks again." Wes drove over to the city offices, spent half an hour being shuffled from one person to the next, and another twenty minutes getting the right person to agree to turn the utilities on that afternoon.

"At least it's today," he sighed, ruffling Kuda's fur back in the truck. With water, heat, light, and some determination and hard work, he could probably get Grandma's house finished and get back to the Black Rock Ranch sooner than he planned. Back to open spaces, no Christmas light overkill, and no tourists.

His determination turned to dismay as he stepped into Grandma's house again. In the daylight, he could see the furniture was old, worn, and as crowded together as the people he'd seen in the streets last night. Knick-knacks filled every available shelf, and the dining table was piled with leaning stacks of paper. There were two open packing boxes in the living room, which multiplied to a dozen when he looked in the bedrooms. It looked like someone had started to pack and had given up.

The entire house had the musty smell of animals, but not urine, thank goodness. Grandma had been particular about her animals. Still, the carpet was worn through in spots, there were cabinets to repair and dingy walls to paint before he could sell it.

So much for finishing the job quickly.

Wes sat bleakly in a chair—after dropping its pile of magazines on the floor—and wondered which room Kuda was sniffing around now. At least somebody was enjoying the state of the house.

He shivered, even in his coat, and whispered a brief prayer for strength before he finally stood. He didn't just need to get started, he needed to move to stay warm. With the house being as cold inside as it was out, he opened all the windows first. Some fresh air would help all the way around.

First, he needed a bed to sleep in. He cleared piles of Grandma's knick-knacks off his old twin bed, but the pictures taped above his dresser brought way too many memories back. Good times with Grandma, hard memories of his dad. And Ellie. His Ellie, who probably wouldn't have married another guy and moved to New York if Wes hadn't taken off after graduation.

He shoved the past back into a corner of his mind and headed for Grandma's room instead. Her bed was mostly clear, and by the time he found sheets in the linen closet, made the bed, and brought his duffel bag in, he was warm again.

"What do you think, Kuda?" he said back in the kitchen. "Time to look in the fridge?" He steeled himself as he opened the door, expecting mold-filled canisters and putrid produce. But some kindly neighbor, maybe Mrs. McCarthy, must have cleaned it out sometime after the funeral. The shelves were clear and the smell was only that of being closed too long.

He left the fridge door open and began searching the cupboards. Dishes, glasses, more dishes; pots and pans and an old Crock Pot; cans of beans, corn, chili, tomato and chicken noodle soup; and finally, to the side of the spice cupboard, a box of baking soda. He ripped the top off and sprinkled it through the fridge, thankful Grandma had taught him a few tricks.

The lights suddenly flickered once, then stayed on. The refrigerator began humming. "What'd'ya know, boy, we've got power!" Wes turned to the sink and ran the tap. Brown, rusty water shot out, but became more clear with every gallon. He turned the thermostat up, and the smell of dusty heat rose from the baseboard units.

"We're in business." He clapped the dust off his hands, hooked his thumbs into his belt, and looked around. "Time to get down to work."

FOUR HOURS LATER, Wes wandered the town square, watching the evening activity and waiting for his styrofoam cup of hot chocolate to cool down. Crowds were gathered around the carousel where the lights were tripled and all its horses and circus animals were decked out in garland. A smaller crowd was gathered to the side of the City Hall door, staring at a decorated window. He studied it as he walked past —a girl lighting candles on a Christmas tree. The translucent colored paper made it look a bit like stained glass and—

His hot chocolate sloshed as he crashed into a walking pile of packages, all over his coat and the sleeve of the person behind the packages.

He dropped his cup and reached out to steady her. One package dropped anyway, and he stooped to collect it from the sidewalk. "Sorry, ma'am, I should have been looking…" His voice trailed off as he looked up.

Ellie McKean. Nine years older, but with the same tousled auburn hair and snappy green eyes. The scattering of year-round freckles across that pert nose hadn't changed either.

She gasped. Opened and closed her mouth.

"I thought you moved away," Wes stammered.

That seemed to pull her together. "I did. I moved back. As you can see." Her clipped voice certainly wasn't welcoming him.

Wes was confused. Sure, he had never made it back to her like he thought he would, but she was the one who got married and left town. Why would she still be mad at him?

He finally found a few words. "I didn't know, Ellie. I haven't been here since the funeral and…"

Her face softened. "I'm sorry about your grandmother, Wes. I know how much she meant to you."

He nodded; he never was sure what to do with sympathy. "I got some time off. I'm clearing out her house."

She frowned and shifted the packages. "Still wandering the country? Haven't settled down yet?"

Wes shrugged. "I'm on a ranch in Colorado, down by Colorado Springs. Been there a couple years."

"Right. That must mean it's about time to move on again." Her voice was bitter.

Again, the confusion. The chimes from the tower clock cut off anything he might say.

"Six-thirty?" Ellie gasped. "I'm late." And she was off,

somehow holding on to her towering stack of purchases and maneuvering around people at the same time.

Of all the things Wes might have expected back in Huckleberry Falls, the mercurial Ellie McKean sure wasn't one of them.

ELLIE BALANCED her packages carefully as she made her way through the crowd. A wire reindeer on top of a Barbie playhouse plus a bag on her arm told her she should have planned better. But mostly she was still in a daze from seeing Wes again.

Nine years. Nine years since he had left her behind in Huckleberry Falls to go explore the world. She knew his grandmother had died and that he'd been home for the funeral and left again, but she had never really expected him to turn up after that.

Of course, that nine years had been filled with her own leaving and coming back, bookending some rotten years she wanted to forget about, but which had also given her a gorgeous, spunky, loving daughter to make her life complete.

Well, almost complete.

Seeing Wes again had made her skin tingle and her heart pound, and all the old rage and frustration had rushed back full force. It seemed she hadn't let go of old feelings after all.

She shoved the memories aside. Right now she needed to focus on getting back to the apartment, hiding the Barbie playhouse, and picking Olivia up from her sister's. She determined to stay pleasant and in control if she ran into Wes again.

. . .

"Mommy!" Six-year-old Olivia cried, throwing herself into her mother's arms. "Look!" She opened her mouth wide and wiggled her front tooth with her tongue. It pivoted forward and back, finally ready to come out.

"It's going to happen tonight, isn't it, sweetie?" Ellie said.

Olivia nodded. "I hope the Tooth Fairy's not too busy to come. You said she might be helping Santa with all his work."

Ellie nuzzled her daughter's neck. "I'm sure she has time for you. Losing a front tooth is an important event, you know."

"You know what else, Mommy? Me and Sarah put all our My Little Ponies in alph-tickle order!" She counted them off on her fingers. "There's Applejack and Celestia and Fluttershy and…"

Ellie nodded, letting Olivia name them all. This daughter of hers never ceased to amaze her. Alpha-tickle order, indeed!

"And Twilight Sparkle's at the end, but she's still at the front of the line 'cause she's the most important." Olivia plastered a kiss on her mother's cheek, and went running off with her four-year-old cousin.

Ellie turned to her sister. "It's been quite a day," she said, flopping in a soft armchair.

Abby put a plate of chicken and mashed potatoes in front of her. "I'm all ears."

Ellie's stomach rumbled at the scent of a delicious dinner. "You didn't have to do this." But she scarfed down a chicken thigh before she spoke again. "Work was actually pretty decent. Alice stayed home with a cold, so she wasn't carping at everyone to bring in more exclusive clients."

"Hallelujah," Abby said, handing her sister a napkin.

Ellie nodded. She loved cutting and styling hair, but the owner of La Chevelure was an expert in making her employees hate their jobs. "So true. Anyway, I also managed to get Olivia's big present home and hidden already, so it's safe from her finding it."

"You hope," Abby said with a knowing smile. "You remember how many presents we 'just stumbled across' as kids, right?"

Ellie nodded in rueful agreement. Maybe she should have taken it to their mother's house until Christmas Eve. Maybe she'd still take it over there. She really wanted to give Olivia a giant surprise on Christmas morning. It would at least be a happier surprise than Ellie herself had received tonight.

"Something wrong with the potatoes?" Abby asked.

"Huh? No, they're perfect."

"You just have that furrow between your brows that you get when you don't like something. If it's not the potatoes, what is it?"

The problem with having an older sister was that she could read your face like no one else. Ellie sighed. "Wes Colton is back in town."

"Wes? No way!" Abby clenched her hands. "Why? After his grandmother died, I expected him never to come back."

"He said something about cleaning out her house."

Abby snorted. "Should have done that a long time ago. Like before *you* came back."

Ellie gave a wan smile. She'd finally given up on her marriage and her husband's New York City high life six months earlier. Marrying Marshall had been a rebound decision if she'd ever heard of one, even if he had been a handsome, high-powered financier who'd swept her off her feet. He'd turned out to be a cad who played around and wanted nothing to do with fatherhood. He'd also turned out to have cutthroat lawyers, so she was back in her hometown with a beloved daughter and good child support, but no other settlement.

She had enough to worry about now, sorting out single parenthood and her career without thinking about her high school sweetheart, no matter how long and lean Wes had looked in those worn Levis, no matter how handsome the planes of his face were under that black Stetson.

"It shouldn't take him long to clear the house out, and he's sure not going to want to stay here. I can avoid him for that long." Ellie muttered.

Abby raised her eyebrows.

Ellie scowled at her and took her plate to the kitchen. "The McKean girls haven't had much luck with love, have we?" she said when she returned with two cups of coffee.

"I don't know if it was bad luck or bad decisions," Abby said. "But I've got Sarah, and her jerk of a father is out of my life for good. I just wish I had the child support you do."

Ellie sat up straighter. "He's not paying again?"

"Nope. He keeps changing jobs, so garnishing his wages doesn't do anything." Abby stirred sugar into her coffee, not meeting Ellie's eyes.

"I'm sorry, Sis." Ellie put her hand on Abby's free arm. "You know we'll help you any way we can."

"I know." Abby swiped at her eyes. "I just hate not being independent."

"You will be. As soon as you get your CPA and become a fantastic forensic accountant. And in the meantime," Ellie raised her cup, "here's to keeping the dirtbags out of our lives." Especially one particular unreliable, cowboy-hatted dirtbag.

ELLIE TUCKED OLIVIA IN, read one more spunky princess story, then kissed her a final time. "I love you, sweetie. Happy dreams."

"You have happy dreams too, Mommy," Olivia said cheerfully, her voice not at all sleepy.

Ellie shook her head and closed the door, retreating to the living room to wait out the time until Olivia wound down enough to sleep. After fifteen minutes with no request for water or the bathroom, there was hope that her daughter had drifted off.

Unfortunately, those fifteen minutes had given Ellie's thoughts time to wander, and her mind, traitorous thing that it was, took a straight path to Wes Colton.

They had spent most of high school glued together. She had helped him with algebra; he'd helped her with memorizing historical dates. She sat in front of him in band, playing the flute to his trumpet. She cheered him on at track meets; he drew her silly pictures. They made oatmeal raisin cookies at his grandmother's, watched bad sci-fi movies at her house, and she listened sympathetically while he complained about the stepmother-from-hell.

Then after they had graduated, when she'd been sure they'd be making wedding plans, Wes had announced that he wanted to explore other places, do other things. That he didn't want to make a commitment he didn't know if he could keep. That he wasn't ready to be tied down.

She'd been sure a lot of that was connected to his dad and stepmother, but she hadn't been able to convince him of that. So he had left, she had cried, and then when she met Marshall...

No. Ellie set her mug down hard. Just because she had a quiet evening didn't mean she had to rethink all her decisions. Wes's unexpected appearance had opened up old wounds, that was all. She could stitch them back up again as easily as she could bandage Olivia's scraped knees. Truly, she could.

She'd be better off turning her thoughts to her career and

how long she could put up with Alice Smith's attitude toward her employees at La Chevelure. The problem was that there were only a few other hair salons in town, and none of them would pay enough for her to meet her bills. Without the resources to open a shop of her own, her original dream, she was stuck where she was.

She sent her thoughts firmly down the familiar worry-paths of finances, career problems, and single-parenthood.

Much easier than thinking about Wes Colton.

2

Ellie held Olivia's hand Saturday as her daughter skipped along in the frosty air, singing a mixed-up combination of Christmas songs and her own words. *We wish you a merry Christmas because little Lord Jesus is asleep in the hay, and I'll go to sleep like baby Jesus so Santa Claus is coming tonight.*

Olivia brought such unbridled joy into her life that Ellie couldn't be sorry for the time she'd spent married to Manipulative Marshall. Well, she really should have given up a couple years earlier, but certainly not before she had Olivia. The girl's zany antics, her boundless enthusiasm, and her random six-year-old kisses kept Ellie going when life seemed hard. And now, with the loose tooth already under her pillow for tonight, Olivia had a slight lisp that made Ellie smile every time she heard it.

On the first day of Christmas, my lovey gave to me a jingle bell, Rudolph red nose. Ellie just shook her head. "I think we need some singing practice time, kiddo," she said. Then she stopped. "No, you know what? I need to teach you a new song."

"Yay! Another song!" Olivia stopped skipping and bounced in place. "Is it about Santa Claus?"

"No, it's just for you." Ellie hunkered down to eye level. "It's called 'All I Want for Christmas is My Two Front Teeth!'"

Olivia clapped a mittened hand over her mouth. "That's going to be my new favorite song!" She pulled Ellie forward, skipping again and singing *my two front teeth, my two front teeth* to her own off-key tune.

Inside the Community Center, the annual Festival of Trees was going strong. Ellie paid for their tickets, and they oohed and aahed their way around the exotically decorated Christmas trees, stopping to look closer at one covered with peacock feathers and another full of red gingham and candy apples.

"Mommy, they have puppies over there!" Olivia pointed.

"They're for people to adopt," Ellie said. "Maybe we can go pet them later, but first I want to find Merry."

"Jesus's mommy?" Olivia asked.

Ellie smiled. "No, my friend Merry Hurst. We work at the salon together, and she's here today doing fancy nails." She picked up Olivia's hand. "Want some sparkly nail polish?"

Olivia grinned, showing off that luscious new gap in her teeth.

They finally found the La Chevelure booth where Merry was busy adding tiny jewels to a client's fingernails, and Coleta had a line of girls waiting for face paint. The Edelweiss ski resort, just north of town, had the booth next to them. A handsome stranger there kept his eye on Merry in between potential customers.

Merry's client held one hand in the light, admiring her finished work. Ellie approached as the woman paid.

"Hey there," Merry said. "How are you two ladies today?"

"I lost a tooth!" Olivia pronounced, grinning to show off

the space. "And Mommy taught me a new song for it." She proceeded to sing the title words at high volume until Ellie put a hand on her shoulder.

"Inside voice, sweetheart. And maybe you can sing it for Merry when you learn it all."

Her eyes were eager. "Could I, Miss Merry?"

Merry nodded, her long brown hair swinging. "If I can paint your fingernails shiny red." She looked at the crowd of people weaving past each other. "I've been swamped all day. You can sit in my chair while I take a potty break, and then we'll do your nails."

Olivia perched on the edge of a folding chair while Ellie sat in another. The man from the Edelweiss booth kept glancing over.

Ellie smiled politely. He was trim, well-dressed and quite good-looking, if you went in for expensive city guys.

When Merry returned, Ellie raised her eyebrows and nodded her head very slightly towards the man.

Merry clamped her lips to keep her smile at bay and mouthed, "Later."

Within five minutes, Olivia had her hands in the air with her fingers spread while she stood in line for face painting. Ellie checked the ski resort guy out again as they waited. She was a little envious of Merry's possibilities.

Possibilities.

Ellie would love to have a new guy around, someone who was kind and loving and trustworthy. Especially if he was the *right* guy. However, with a child and a full time job, she didn't know how to make it happen. *If* she could even meet someone that might qualify—not an easy task in a tourist town. She knew just about everyone who lived in Huckleberry Falls, and she'd already made the massive mistake of risking her heart on a stranger.

Not going to happen again. She was fine being single—
she had Olivia and her mother and Abby. What more did she
need?

Once Olivia had a candy cane painted on her cheek, they
went to see the puppies for adoption. Ellie stayed firm as her
daughter kept begging to take one home. "We don't have
room in the apartment," was her standard answer. The truth
was, she'd love to have a pet, but life was too unsettled now.
Maybe when she was able to move them into a house.

Olivia gave a goodbye squeeze to a fuzzy golden retriever
pup, and they browsed booths together. Books, handcrafts,
artwork, jewelry. Everywhere they went, Olivia showed off the
gap in her smile. She had just finished singing her "All I Want
for Christmas" phrase to the quilt lady when Ellie heard a
deep, rumbly voice behind her.

"She's pretty cute," Wes said.

Ellie froze. She did *not* want to turn around to see him.

Olivia had different ideas, however. "Hi! I'm Olivia and
I'm six and I lost another tooth."

"I see that," he said.

"Who are you?" she asked.

Ellie put a hand on Olivia's shoulder, still not meeting
Wes's eyes. "You're not supposed to talk to strangers,
remember, sweetie?"

"But Mommy, if he tells me his name, he won't be a
stranger!"

Ellie sighed. They had relaxed so much being back home
that Olivia had forgotten all the New York rules. Which
should still apply, no matter how safe Huckleberry Falls felt.

Not that Ellie was relaxed any more. Christmas carols
might be playing overhead, friends might be greeting friends
with hugs, but she was stuck standing next to her old high
school sweetheart.

"Wes." She couldn't help the way her voice sounded short and clipped.

"Ellie," he responded with a much warmer tone.

"We, uh, have to go. We're late."

He raised his eyebrows. She determined not to look at those dark chocolate eyes, the ones that had always been able to read her moods.

"What in the world could you be late for? It's Saturday, and you're wandering around a Christmas festival." His mouth crooked up, which was just as dangerous. "Is this your daughter?"

Olivia was looking between the two, watching both their faces. "Mommy?" she asked, tugging on Ellie's shirt. "Is he a stranger?"

Ellie closed her eyes and prayed for patience. "No, honey, he's someone I knew a long time ago."

"We could change that to someone you know now," Wes said with a smile.

Ellie jerked her head up. "You left me once, Wes. I'm not about to let it happen again."

"No forgiveness, huh? Not even for clueless adolescents who grew up?"

His eyes pierced her, looked right through her defenses. Right to the heart that still thrummed for him like it never had for Marshall, if she were honest. His scrawny teenage frame had filled out with ranch-worked muscles to the point that…well, if she were Abby, she'd be fanning herself.

She steeled herself against the rising feelings. She had a daughter to protect and a life to rebuild. "Maybe adolescents deserve forgiveness, but you still haven't grown up, have you, Wes? Still moving around instead of making a commitment to anything?"

He had the grace to look embarrassed. While he gazed

down at his worn cowboy boots, Ellie took Olivia's hand. "We have to go now."

"But Mommy, I didn't show him my missing tooth!" Olivia's tug on her hand was surprisingly strong.

Ellie rolled her eyes. "Okay, you can show him, and then we're leaving."

The six-year-old turned immediately to the cowboy and bared her teeth. "See, Mr. Wes! The tooth fairy might bring me a dollar!"

"I see," Wes said as Ellie pulled Olivia away. She didn't care how much her body longed for a hug from this lean, rugged man. Didn't care that it looked like he wanted to pick up where they left off. It was his fault they "left off" in the first place!

Nope. No way would Wes Colton impact her life again. The sooner he packed up his grandmother's house and went back to his ranch, the better.

***

WES KEPT his eyes on Ellie and her daughter as long as he could, until they were lost in the crowd.

Grandma's conspiratorial gossip had told him Ellie had married and moved back East, but Wes had no idea she'd come back to Huckleberry until last night. No idea what happened to her marriage. And no idea about her impish daughter.

Even at six, the daughter's smile reminded him of Ellie's as a teenager. Of Ellie's as he'd like to see her again—carefree and loving.

From her reaction, though, it didn't look like carefree and loving were in the cards. He wasn't sure why. He'd missed her an awful lot when he'd left, but the excitement of new horizons had taken over. And she'd obviously moved on— she'd gone and married someone else.

His heart had broken a bit when he'd heard about her marriage, but he could only blame himself. If he hadn't been in such an all-fired rush to get out of their small town and into the bigger world...

He'd dated since then, without realizing that he'd been measuring every woman against her. It was no wonder nothing ever worked out.

And now? Even though they were both single, she was doing a good job of shutting him out.

Wes reminded himself that her attitude shouldn't be a problem at all—he was here to clean out Grandma's house, get it up for sale, and head back to the Black Rock ranch. He had a load of work ahead of him and no time for a romance anyway.

But his shoulders sagged, and his heart suddenly felt dull, like it would never pound with excitement again.

He took his cowboy hat off and reshaped it with shaking hands. Then he planted it firmly back on his head. He had no business at a light-hearted Christmas festival when there was work to be done.

BACK AT GRANDMA'S, Kuda greeted Wes with a lick and a talkative howl. Wes sang back to him for a minute, then looked around with a critical eye. He'd sorted papers upon papers that morning and couldn't face any more of it. In the meantime...

Under all the knickknacks, Grandma had some pretty decent furniture. Well-built and still solid, handed down through a generation or two. It was worth keeping, as long as you weren't a nomad like Wes. What was he supposed to do with china hutches and bedroom suites?

That gave him a good starting point, though. He took large garbage bags and began sorting through the two bedroom dressers. Some of Grandma's clothes were worn and faded and should have been thrown out years ago. Some could be donated, as long as people didn't care about the latest fashions.

Wes blanched at the first drawer: underwear, of course. Did thrift stores even take used underwear? He shook his head at the thought and tossed it all in the garbage pile. The other drawers were easier, and he moved on to the closet.

An hour later, he had a massive pile of full bags in the garage, waiting for the garbage truck, and a smaller pile in the living room to donate. He polished the dressers and the bed and admired the gleam. Did hundred-year-old furniture qualify as antique? He should get Mrs. Abernathy from the antique store to come out.

In the meantime, he rolled his eyes at the ugly lamp on Grandma's bedside table. Bold green glass with yellow and orange bits, and a brown metal base. What kind of decor would that go with, anyway? Something from the Seventies? The tasseled floor lamp in the living room was almost as bad —he much preferred a plain white lampshade.

"I know you loved it, Grandma," he said, glaring at the green lamp, "and you said it was a family heirloom, but that family's all gone, and I think it's just clunky. You wouldn't mind if I sold it, would you?"

No answer. Not that he expected one, but Grandma had been on his mind all through the clothes-sorting.

What would Grandma think of all this? When he'd visited back in January, a month before she died, she hadn't really recognized him. He believed she was in a better place now, that she had her mind back and wasn't scared any more, but would she really care what he did with her earthly possessions?

He snorted. Grandma had a few things that were important to her, but people had always been more precious than belongings. He ought to be more concerned over what she'd think of his life.

They had grieved together after his mom—her daughter—had died when he was ten, and then Grandma had stepped in to fill that role as only a grandmother could. Then when his dad took up with Bimbo Barbie as Wes was starting high school, Grandma was there to fill in the gaps. It hadn't taken long before he'd moved in with her.

She had always supported him, gone to all his events, encouraged him to do his best, taught him that who he was inside was far more important than what he did. She'd been happy for him when he'd found a place on that first ranch.

Wes's mind shifted uncomfortably. She'd been happy for him, yes. But she'd also patted his hand and said, "You'll find your place someday." He'd never wanted to think too hard about what that meant, but now the phrase kept rattling around in his brain.

Had she meant ranching *wasn't* his place? He'd been at four ranches now, but he'd settled well at Black Rock. He enjoyed working with the livestock, especially the horses. He liked being outside all day, didn't really even mind the winter snow or summer heat. But had Grandma thought he should be doing something else?

He snorted. Nothing like getting the same ambiguous comments from two completely different people. Uncle Dirt, an old guy on the Black Rock ranch who claimed his nickname by being "older than dirt," had told him basically the same thing. "You're good at this, son, but this isn't where you belong. You keep looking."

Uncle Dirt carried a lot of wisdom behind his sun-browned skin. He'd been right about the one girl Wes had dated for more than a week, and right when one cowboy mistreated the horses. He knew what it took to be a ranch hand and could pick who would stay and who would leave within a day of them starting work.

Wes had stayed, but if Grandma and Uncle Dirt were right, and Wes wasn't a ranch hand, what was he? He was well into adulthood and had nothing beyond his high school diploma, no experience with anything but animals, and an aversion to working in an office. There were other outdoor jobs, sure, but somehow working as a ski lift operator at the Edelweiss Resort didn't do anything for him.

He let out a grumpy sigh, shrugged into his coat, and called Kuda for a walk. The wind was whipping, but he needed to get away from the responsibility of the house and the weight of his questions.

3

"It's quite busy for us now," Mrs. Abernathy at the antique store said on Monday. "Ms. Schmidt is out with the flu, and I don't have anybody else I can leave the store with. Would you have pictures, by any chance?"

Hallelujah, Wes had done something right. "Just the stuff I got cleaned up," he said, pulling up the photos on his phone. "I think they got the china hutch when they got married in the fifties, but I remember her saying that the bed had been her grandmother's. Or maybe her great-grandmother's—I can't really remember."

Mrs. Abernathy nodded as she examined each picture, her face not showing anything. It made Wes nervous, but not as nervous as when he glanced out the window and saw Ellie.

She wasn't walking by; she was just standing by the big front window. Why?

Mrs. Abernathy nodded. "I'd have to see them to be sure, but it looks like the hutch is mid-century modern like you expected. I can't tell with the bed—I'd have to check for maker's marks. But this chest of drawers—it has an age and patina I don't normally see. It could still be a reproduction, or it could be a true Shaker and worth some money."

"There's a roll-top desk and a rocking chair, and some other stuff I can't think of right now."

"You say you're putting the house on the market?"

"Yes, ma'am." He glanced back out at Ellie, who was now looking in at him.

"Will you be in town long?"

Wes twisted his Stetson in his hands. "Can't rightly say. Just as long as it takes to get things sorted out. I'm supposed to be back in Colorado by Christmas."

She handed him the phone back. "I'll try to get out there some evening, if I'm not too worn out. But it would be eight or nine o'clock."

She took down his contact information. "Set aside whatever else she had that you want me to look at—silver, collectibles, that sort of thing. I can go through them at the same time."

"Yes, ma'am. I'll talk to you soon." He took a deep breath before he turned to the door and faced whatever Ellie wanted. She was obviously waiting for him, but he couldn't think what she'd want. She certainly hadn't been overly welcoming at the Festival of Trees.

He pushed through to the cold, buttoning his coat as the wind hit him. "Ellie?" he said.

"Wes. I was heading out to get a sandwich—it's my lunch break—and I saw you. And it seemed perfect, but I don't know if you'll want to, but—" She was twisting the strap of her purse into knots.

He'd never known her to be so flustered. "Ellie, you're rambling. Start at the beginning. And let's get out of this wind."

"I was headed down to Soupçon."

"Soup's On?"

Ellie giggled at his misunderstanding. "Yeah, a lunch spot just down here."

"Hang on a sec." Wes went to his truck to give Kuda a treat. "You stay here and be good, boy. I'll be back in just a bit."

"He's beautiful," Ellie said from behind his shoulder. "Have you had him long?"

"A couple of years. My life is kinda quiet." He couldn't very well say that Kuda kept him from getting too lonely, that it was nice to have someone to talk to in the evenings.

They started walking, hunched into their coats, their puffs of breath leading the way. "The thing is," Ellie began, "my uncle broke his leg skiing yesterday. He was practicing for the Santa Chase. He hit some ice on a turn and tumbled badly coming down the Zurich run."

"He'll be off his feet for a while." Wes sympathized. Being laid up was no fun.

"That's the problem." Ellie turned into Soupçon, and the warm air hit them like a tropical storm. Wes's stomach growled.

Ellie smirked. "Still a walking appetite, I see."

He managed not to roll his eyes. He didn't eat like he had as a teenager, but he was used to a lot of food to fuel him through the long days. This morning's cereal and coffee just didn't compare. "The problem?" he prodded.

"You know my Uncle Steve's Trails' End Stables, right?"

"Of course. So he needs help taking care of the horses?"

"*Urgh.* Let me finish, would you?" She glared at him, and it sent him back to the time when that stare would lead to him kissing her cute nose.

"Don't look at me like that!" She didn't stamp her foot

like she used to. Instead, the chill from outside seemed to have enveloped them again.

Wes schooled his face as she continued. "Uncle Steve provides sleigh rides around town for the tourists. He can't do it now, obviously, but the town counts on it. Some people come just for the sleigh rides."

Wes stiffened, knowing what was coming. "I suppose he wears a Santa suit?"

"No, just his big coat. He also has a thick rug to keep him warm, plus one for the tourists."

That was something, anyway. A man could work outside with no problem, but just sitting in the cold was another story. And a Santa suit would have made it a no-go.

Ellie looked at him with expectant eyes.

"Well?" he asked. He wasn't going to pass up the opportunity for some light teasing. Maybe it would make her soften a bit.

"You're going to make me say it, aren't you? Going to make me grovel when I ask, too?"

Wes saw a bit of a twinkle in her expression, so he lifted one eyebrow and let it drop. "Now that you mention it…"

"Wes Colton!" Her green eyes flashed, and her mouth gave a hint of a quirk. "Okay, then. Will you *pleeease* consider taking over the sleigh rides for Uncle Steve? Nobody else can do it during the day, and he'll be able to trust the horses with you."

Wes considered. Besides helping Ellie and her uncle, it might not be a bad thing. He was going to go crazy if all he did was sort through Grandma's stuff for days on end, no matter how much he wanted to get back to the ranch. And he wouldn't have to spend the day in a Santa suit. "Daytime only?"

Ellie nodded. "Ten until dusk."

SLEIGH RIDE WITH THE COWBOY

Not good. That would only leave him the evenings at Grandma's, which probably wouldn't be enough to get the job done and get him back to the ranch for Christmas. Not unless he just threw things away willy-nilly, and Grandma wouldn't like that one bit. "Tell you what. I'll go out and talk to him tonight, see what we can work out."

"Thanks, Wes! I knew you would!" Ellie's arms were suddenly around him in a hug.

He almost froze at her mixed signals, but Wes Colton was no one's fool. If he had a beautiful woman in his arms, he was going to take advantage of it. He held her to him, inhaled the scent of her hair, then sighed in resignation as she stepped back.

"Uh, sorry," she stammered, blushing as strongly as she ever had. "I shouldn't have done that. You do know it was only relief and 'thank you,' don't you?"

His arms felt emptier than ever. Once, she had been all he'd wanted in life. He'd moved on since then—he'd had to. But for a moment his soul had cried out that she was still the one.

"I really do need to get lunch," she said, motioning to the counter.

He nodded, but couldn't manage anything more.

"Do you want anything?"

He shook his head and watched as she got in line. Maybe he hadn't just been missing Grandma or feeling homesick for Huckleberry Falls. Maybe he'd been homesick for *her*.

It didn't matter. Wes had obligations now. He wasn't staying in town.

Ellie McKean was a distraction he didn't need.

ELLIE WASHED Cleo's long hair with a touch of envy. The luscious feel of thick curls and the ability to put it up in elegant styles was one of her teenage dreams that had never really gone away.

She sighed. Short and sassy was the look for her right now —she didn't have time for anything fancy. Hers wasn't quite wash-and-go, but it only took a little styling gel on her natural curls to look good.

She worked conditioner into Cleo's hair, giving a scalp massage that left the young woman sighing in pleasure. Ellie smiled. Some people came just for that. If she could teach people how to do that for their spouses, there would be a lot of happy marriages out there.

Alice Smith, the owner, sidled up. "You need to get a move on!" she groused in Ellie's ear. "Mrs. Milakovic's here already. And she's *important!*"

Ellie set her jaw as Alice left. All her clients were important, to her at least, and Mrs. Milakovic was known for arriving early. She was also kind and patient. Ellie finished the scalp massage in her own time, rinsed Cleo's hair, and sent her off to her station while she cleaned up and had a word with Mrs. M.

"I know I'm early," Mrs. Milakovic said with a smile, "but I can't escape my mother's training. You take your time—I brought a book."

Ellie thanked her and returned to her station. She didn't chat with Cleo as much as she might have, but she didn't shave a single minute off what was necessary to give her a good cut and style. If her boss didn't like it, she could go jump in the lake. And freeze solid, for all Ellie cared.

Alice was enough to try anyone's patience. Everything centered around the money a stylist brought in and the prestige of having high-end clients. Alice wanted to be part of the elite social circle, and heaven forbid the salon should have its chairs filled with run-of-the-mill town residents.

Most of the other stylists were getting fed up, too. Coleta had even found an ad in *Cosmetology News* for a manager for "a top salon in Huckleberry Falls, Wyoming." They had chattered over which salon it might be, but no one really had the experience to apply, although Ellie had some management classes under her belt.

Ellie brought Mrs. Milakovic back. Ellie liked her and wouldn't mind using her as a role model. Mrs. M served on the board of a dozen charities and was a lot less stuck-up than Alice herself. "Same thing today, or would you like to try something different?" Ellie asked.

"Just a touch up, please," Mrs. Milakovic said, fingering her ash-blonde hair. "And perhaps a little shorter this time."

"About to here?" Ellie motioned with her finger.

The older woman smiled. "Ellie, you've been doing my hair since Rebecca moved away, and you've never done me wrong. You look at my face shape and decide where it will fall the best."

Ellie smiled. This was what she loved about her job—clients who trusted her, and who loved the way they looked when they walked out.

When she finished, she accepted an air kiss and warm goodbye from Mrs. M, then went back to clean her station.

Alice gripped her arm, stopping her broom in mid-stroke. "You kept her waiting for twenty minutes! That's unacceptable!"

Ellie stared at her boss. "What would you have me do? Leave Cleo with wet hair and no cut? I can't help it if Mrs. Milakovic gets here so early."

"You could at least go out and greet her," Alice growled.

"I did. She was very pleasant and said she was fine with her book."

"*Hmmph.*" Alice stomped off to find someone else to torment. Merry Hurst, from the look of it. Alice had been trying to get Merry to do nails instead of hair, but Merry wasn't having any of it.

If Ellie had any other salon to work at, she would. Quick Clips was a no appointment, cut-it-quick sort of place— definitely not the type of career change she wanted. Joanna's catered to old ladies wanting perms and sets, and Hair Today had no stylist openings.

She earned a good bit at La Chevelure, and that plus the child support her lawyer had wrangled in the divorce settlement, cleverly set up with payment arrangements that Marshall couldn't avoid, was enough that she didn't stress over the bills each month. Unfortunately, she had signed a pre-nup before she married Marshall, which gave her no settlement for herself. No lump sum to put toward her dream of owning her own salon.

And what now? She'd been back in Huckleberry Falls for nearly six months and loved being near her mother and sister. She didn't want to move to Cheyenne or Denver where there were larger markets, but could she stand to work for Alice Smith forever? And while she wasn't ready for a serious romance yet, she would like to date once in a while.

The problem was that she wouldn't let a tourist into her life again, and she knew the guys in town too well—there wasn't anybody she really wanted to spend time with.

Her breath caught. She shoved the thoughts away, but they kept coming back.

Wes was here.

Ellie swept cut hair into a pile.

He was oh-so-handsome as a rugged cowboy.

Ellie growled as she overshot the dust pan and hair scattered into the aisle.

Her heart still pounded when she saw him.

No! She wasn't going down that road again.

She swept properly and slammed the trashcan as she dumped the hair in. Wes had hurt her just as much as Marshall had. Maybe even more, because it was her broken heart from Wes that had pushed her into Marshall's arms.

Ellie and Wes had been friends, not just boyfriend/girlfriend. They had grown up together, laughed at movies together, sang songs and practiced dancing together.

She relived that last kiss, his arms around her, her hands in his hair, his mouth on hers. She had felt safe, loved, complete. It should have lasted forever.

But Wes had suddenly latched on to some idealistic idea of a travelling cowboy's life, and Ellie hadn't been enough to keep him in Huckleberry Falls.

She stepped on her mental brakes and planted those memories firmly in a hidden corner of her mind, replacing them with thoughts of her daughter. One more hair cut to go, and she'd pick Olivia up from daycare. Her gapped-tooth smile, happy chatter, and off-key song mash-ups would shake Ellie out of this mood. They'd have the six-year-old's favorite fish sticks for dinner, read some books, and maybe paint pink sparkles on Olivia's toenails before bed.

Olivia was what she needed to focus on, not bygone days that could never be again.

4

Wes drove into Trail's End Stables with Kuda panting on the seat beside him. After four days in a house with a tiny yard, the Husky was excited to go anywhere.

The stable block covered a good bit of ground, though not nearly as much as the main buildings at the Black Rock Ranch. Steve's front building held about twenty stalls, if he remembered rightly, and it looked like he had added more stalls along the side of his indoor arena. Some led out to small paddocks, and behind the outdoor arena were about forty acres in divided pasture, with another hundred or so for hay.

"Stay here, boy," he told Kuda. "Don't know if you'll be welcome or not."

Wes stepped down from the truck, buttoning his old Carhartt coat as he walked. The barn was empty of people, but full of horses. A bay in the first stall stuck his head over the half-door and nickered, setting several of the others into a frenzy of whinnying.

He walked down the aisle, speaking quietly to the horses and admiring the care given. Well-oiled leather halters hung outside each stall, along with a lead rope for each. The horses stood on fresh shavings; the aisle had been swept clear of any spilled hay and grain.

A young woman loped a sorrel Quarter Horse smoothly around a set of cones in the arena. When she slowed to a walk, Wes called out. "Is Steve Mitchell around?"

"Up at the house, I think," she answered. "He got hurt yesterday."

Wes nodded his thanks and returned through the barn to knock on the back door of the house.

"Come in, whoever you are!" a voice rang out.

Wes let himself in through a mudroom filled with rubber boots, cowboy boots, and old coats, and followed the voice through the kitchen to a sitting room.

The carpet was worn, a saddle lay on an armchair, and the couch had a saddle blanket over one end. Steve McKean lay against it, looking pretty much how Wes remembered him, with the addition of a scruffy beard and a bright white cast that contrasted with the dusty, horsey feel of the room. A pair of aluminum crutches lay on the floor alongside.

"Come on in," Steve said. "I sure can't get up to greet you." He studied his visitor. "Wes Colton. Haven't seen you around here since your Grandma's passing. What can I do for you?"

Wes moved the saddle to the floor and sat in the armchair, hat in his hands. "Actually, it's what I can do for you instead. Ellie told me you got hurt."

Steve glared at his cast. "Can't even put pants on," he grumbled. "And the doc wants me to keep it up as much as possible. 'Course, it hurts like the dickens if I stand up, so that part's not hard."

"You got somebody to take care of the horses?"

"Yeah, the guy that mucks out stalls in the morning is

coming early to feed them, and I have someone else to do the evening."

Wes rotated the brim of his Stetson. "So you're all set?"

"I'm not dead—I can still take care of things. Except…" He pinned Wes with a look. "Ellie sent you out here about the sleigh rides, didn't she?" He set his jaw. "Interfering young woman."

Wes lifted one shoulder. "She said people counted on them, and you wouldn't be able to do it. So she asked if I could." But his mind was stuck back on Steve's grumbling—it was all Ellie's idea. Did that mean she was starting to trust him again?

"Huh. You always did like horses," Steve said. "Your grandma said you're a cowboy now?"

"I guess you could say that. I'm a hand on the Black Rock Ranch, outside Colorado Springs, worked a couple different ranches before that. Do a little bit of everything—moving herds, mending fences, branding."

"You ever driven a horse before? Sleigh or buggy?"

"Mostly we use four-wheelers anywhere a buggy could go. But the guy that ran one of the other ranches liked to keep a team in use. I drove a pair of Belgians a few times pulling the old hay wagon, and once or twice with the sleigh for his grandkids."

Steve nodded. "It'll do. Sadie's a good old mare, but there's a trick to driving, especially turning, that you don't get from a saddle. Tell you what. You go on out to the barn and look around. Old Sadie's probably out in one of the paddocks still—not feeding time yet—but if Carolyn is riding like she usually is, she can introduce you. Then come back and we'll talk some more."

Wes settled his hat back on his head and went back to the barn. The sorrel was getting a rubdown, and his rider turned out to be Carolyn. "I'll just be another minute," she said.

While he waited, Wes poked his head into the tack room and found the harness hanging on the wall. Several tidy grooming boxes were on the floor beneath a double row of saddle racks. He wondered where Steve kept the sleigh.

Hoof steps clattered on the cement aisle and Wes went back out. When the sorrel was settled in his stall, Carolyn took Wes out to the paddocks. "Sadie's the brown mare over there," she said, pointing to a cluster of horses nibbling at the dry grass poking through the layer of snow. A bay gelding stood dozing next to her, and a palomino pony grazed close by.

"She's a sweetheart," Carolyn said. "What are you going to do?"

Wes didn't quite chuckle. "I might be doing the sleigh rides while Steve is laid up?"

Carolyn brightened. "I'm so glad! My kids love to go each year, and I thought I'd have to break the bad news to them."

"We still have to work out the details, so don't say anything to them yet," Wes warned.

Carolyn nodded and said goodbye. "Time to get home before the kids do."

Wes tipped his hat and went out to meet his new equine partner. Sadie turned her big rump around willingly, then nuzzled him as he brought a sugar cube out of his pocket.

She had a rather homely face, but she was calm and personable. He scratched behind one ear, rubbed her face, then headed back to the house.

Steve was up on his crutches trying to get a glass of water. One crutch fell, and Wes picked it up.

"I thought you were supposed to stay down," Wes said, handing it to him and taking the glass.

Steve settled the crutch under his arm and made his way back to the couch. "Doctors are always too cautious. They'd keep you wrapped in cotton until you were fully healed if they had their way." He thanked Wes for the water. "So what do you think?"

"Sadie seems like a sweetheart. Easy to manage, but not asleep."

"She'll see you straight, will Sadie," Steve said. "She's getting on in years, but she's still well-muscled and she's steady around people and noises.

Wes nodded. "What hours do the sleigh rides run?"

"Ten in the morning until about five. Getting too dark after that. I take 'em around two sides of the town square—don't want to tie traffic up too much—and then down Third Street where there are a lot of Christmas decorations in yards, then around the yellow Victorian and back. Takes about twenty minutes."

Wes calculated the time to get Sadie out there and hitched and bring her back again, and added it up. "With all the prep needed, that's more time than I can rightly do. Any possibility of adjusting things? Say, maybe start at noon?"

Steve swirled the ice in his glass and gave Wes a rueful smile. "Son, any time you have will work for me. If you weren't here, we'd have to cancel them completely. I wouldn't trust any of the old coots with a horse in harness."

Wes chuckled. "One more question. Is Sadie good around dogs? I've got a Husky who would love to go with me."

"Shouldn't be a problem. She used to work alongside cattle dogs."

Wes grinned and shook Steve's hand. Hopefully splitting the work at Grandma's house between morning and evening, with some much-needed horse time between, would keep him sane and still let him get back to the ranch for Christmas.

On the other hand, maybe he could even set an evening or two aside for some fun, if he could get Ellie to go out with him again. Nothing serious, nothing to keep him there more than an extra day. Just some time to maybe become friends again.

ELLIE STARED AT ALICE, shocked at what her boss was demanding. "I can't. I have to pick my daughter up."

"And my son," Merry added.

Alice Smith simply shook her head. "You'll just have to make other arrangements. I've been dying to get Laura Thornton on our customer list for a long time, and now she wants to come with her mother and sister. I'll do Laura myself. Ellie, you take the mother, and Merry, you take the sister."

"What about Coleta? Isn't she working tonight?" Merry asked.

"She's not experienced enough." She looked at the two of them. "Well, go on. Surely you have plenty of family around to take care of your children."

Alice strode away, leaving Ellie and Merry dumbfounded.

"She can't do that!"

"She just did."

Ellie growled to herself. "Mom won't be off work in time. Neither will Abby."

"I can call my mom," Merry said. "Unless she's on a tight deadline for a client, she's always up for kids in the house." Merry's mother was a top dress designer, but running her own business did give her some leeway.

Merry made arrangements for the children, but Ellie's anger only dropped from a boil to a strong simmer. "I can't do this much longer. She's horrible to work for, but there's no place else I can go."

"There's always Quick Clips." Merry chuckled.

"Whoa—not that desperate! I'm just glad my attorney pinned my ex down for child support the way he did. If he could come up with an actual settlement for me, a good one, I could start my own salon." Ellie looked around to make sure Alice hadn't reappeared. Coleta was the only stylist half-listening, but Merry told her everything anyway.

Merry, though, looked shocked. "You'd do that? Do you realize how much work owning a business is?"

She knew. She'd been researching and talking to salon owners off and on for the last nine years. "I would be working for *me*. I'd be in charge of what happens in my life, not depending on someone else's whims or bad moods. Or their unreasonable demands."

Merry eyed her speculatively. "I've watched Mom with her business, and no way would I want all that on me." She stroked the smooth lavender polish on her nails, then tapped her finger against her chin. "If you had a partner to help with the financing, would you do it? I mean, are you serious, or is this just a dream you've been thinking about?"

Ellie blinked slowly, not sure she was understanding what Merry was saying. "A partner? You?"

"Maybe. I still have Ray's life insurance to invest, but right now, I only want to cut hair, not run a business. My clients would come with me if I moved, though."

"Oh." Ellie deflated a little. A partner would make a big difference in achieving her dream, but if Merry didn't want to...

But then why did she bring it up?

"I wouldn't mind being a silent partner," Merry added,

her eyes twinkling. "If you found the right spot for a new salon…"

Her own salon. Her big life goal since she went to cosmetology school. A salon that would be hers to create the way she wanted. Hers to manage, to welcome every client, not just the prestigious ones. Hers to add some compassion to the management.

She turned back to Merry, stammering. "I think…oh wow… Are you sure?"

Merry grinned. "You'd have to have all the pieces in place, and you'd need to get a business plan past my mother—I'd want her to be my advisor on whether to jump in or not. But yes, I'm serious."

Ellie bit the side of her thumb, trying not to actually jump in excitement. "I think I've got rather a lot of planning to do. And thank you!"

Ellie wandered through the salon while she waited for the Thorntons to come in. She studied the layout of the stylist stations and tried to imagine different configurations and what would work best. She perused the shelves of high-end product and considered which brands she would carry herself. She walked past Alice's office and surreptitiously glanced in— the owner was frowning over a printout with a lot of numbers. Yes, she'd need to look at the financial workings closely. When she got back to the hair-washing stations, she knew she'd want an area with quieter colors and dimmer lighting, but she'd keep the layout—it was perfect to spend an extra few minutes giving a client a scalp massage.

The front door chimed, and she cut off her planning. She, Merry and Alice arrived at the lobby together, with Alice plastering a gracious smile on her face. Couldn't anybody see how fake she was?

• • •

Sitting in side-by-side salon chairs, Laura Thornton and her sister wanted simple trims. Merry and Alice got right to the shampoos and head massages, but the senior Mrs. Thornton grinned at Ellie.

"I am sick and tired of long waves, and I'm feeling too old for them anyway." She eyed Ellie in the mirror. "I want something like yours."

"You'd look great with shorter hair," Ellie said. "But what specifically do you like about mine? Would you like to look at some books for other ideas?"

Mrs. Thornton shook her head. "This is a whim. Give me something fun and flirty."

This could go very well or very badly, but Ellie loved the challenge to prove herself. She ran her fingers through her new client's hair. Thick, full, slightly coarse. She studied her face shape in the mirror—Mrs. Thornton's square jaw could be softened with the right cut, and her high forehead was perfect for light bangs.

"Okay, then," Ellie said. "Truthfully, a cut like mine wouldn't work on you—your hair is wonderfully thick and a bit heavy, while mine is fine and fly-away. But we can cut it to about here," she motioned with her finger, "use layers to lighten it, and give you some piece-y bangs."

"Would it be hard to style?"

Ellie shook her head. "You could curl it for a light-hearted look, or just blow-dry it smooth and it will settle neatly and look quite different."

Mrs. Thornton grinned. The others came back and settled in for their cuts while Ellie and the older woman went to shampoo.

Mrs. Thornton sighed in delight at her scalp massage and jokingly asked for twenty minutes more. But the most fun was the look her daughter gave her as Ellie began cutting off long lengths.

"Mom! Tell her to stop!"

"No way, Laura. I'm getting out of my rut and having some fun."

With the help of the blow dryer, curling iron, and some stiff product, Ellie brought Mrs. Thornton back to the lobby with a cute, slightly-curly bob that stopped just above her chin. Laura was speechless, but the sister said, "Mom, that's gorgeous!"

Mrs. Thornton smiled and sent her curls dancing. "I have a new favorite stylist," she exclaimed.

"I'm glad you like it," Ellie said. She kept her smile calm, but pride and satisfaction bubbled up inside her. *This* was what kept her going. "Shall we set an appointment in about six weeks?" She rang up Mrs. Thornton and scheduled her return, then went back to clean up, glad the evening was finally over.

Ellie passed Alice's office on the way, noting that her boss was once again frowning over papers. Oh well, not her problem. *Her* problem would be the delightful one of searching out an available storefront.

"Let's finish up and go get the kids," she told Merry.

5

W es clucked to Sadie, and the mare moved off, sprightly despite her age. Kuda settled on the seat beside him while the two women in back giggled. "I've always wanted to do this, but George is such a stick in the mud. Snow means skiing to him, nothing else."

Wes pointed out the carousel in the town square as he passed it, and told about the Advent windows like the one they'd seen at City Hall. "It's a Swiss tradition called *Adventfester*. People create colored-paper Christmas scenes in November, block the windows so no one can see, and a new one gets lit each night until Christmas Eve. They look like stained glass windows. The tenth one will be revealed at dusk tonight." Not that he would have known that before, but driving tourists around meant he'd had to prepare for a lot of questions.

"What a quaint idea," the other woman exclaimed. "We could probably entice the men with drinks after the tour. Do you take people to see them in the sleigh?"

Wes turned his head slightly. "I'm sorry, no. Sleigh rides

are strictly daytime. We'll pass one or two soon, but the best time to see them is at night."

He could feel the woman's frown, but he wasn't going to keep the mare out late after a full day's work, and he didn't trust tourists, fast cars, monster trucks, and headlights to keep them safe.

His tour day filled with a dad and two kids, three sisters together, and a retired couple, all providing great eavesdropping entertainment. Several romantic couples, on the other hand, gave him plenty of time to think. Would Ellie like a sleigh ride? Had she ever gone on one with her uncle driving?

It didn't strike him as a great date during the daytime, though, even if they had a day off from work. And he wasn't a good enough skier to want to go on a torchlight run. So what would she think was fun besides the bowling they'd done as teens?

He had enough downtime between tourists to feed Sadie some grain and brush her lightly around the harness leather. He glanced over at Ellie's salon. He couldn't see her station from outside, but there was a constant stream of clients, and he imagined she'd be exhausted when she finished. Maybe just a movie? Something she didn't have to dress up for?

Through the rest of the afternoon, Wes puzzled over the conundrum of where to take her and if she'd even agree to come. He threw out several ideas as just plain lame, and still hadn't come to a conclusion by the time he pulled the trailer back into Steve's.

A white pickup lined with dozens of compartments sat in front of the barn—the vet was here. Wes unloaded Sadie, groomed her and put her away, then went to see what was happening.

Steve leaned on his crutches outside a stall, while Dr. Janssen tried to examine a skittish gelding.

"Should you be out here, Steve?" Wes asked. "Can I help?"

Steve took a breath in relief. "I'm glad you're back. And no, I shouldn't be out here, but I didn't have a choice. Doctoring Comet in his stall isn't working so well, though. Can you put him in cross-ties? And be ready to twitch him if necessary? Seems I'm pretty useless."

Wes motioned for Kuda to lay down next to the tack room, then brought the gelding out of his stall. He soothed him with a low murmur of words, clipping leads on either side of his halter to keep him centered in the aisle.

"I need to stitch up his stifle, but it's a two person job," Dr. Janssen said. "I can't even get him to stand for the anesthetic."

Steve handed Wes the twitch, a long, jointed aluminum thing to go on a horse's top lip that would let him put anything from gentle pressure to an extremely strong pinch on it. Wes didn't care for them, and if he twitched a horse at all, he preferred just to hold it lightly and jiggle it to keep the horse's attention on him, not on whatever a vet or farrier was doing.

Now, though, Comet only seemed to need someone at his head to murmur softly and keep a steady hand on his neck. He jerked his foot up in reaction to the anesthetic needle, but soon became numb enough to nuzzle Wes's pocket while Dr. Janssen put six stitches in.

After a penicillin jab, Wes walked the gelding back to his stall, looking in satisfaction at the clean shavings in his stall. Steve ran his stable well.

"You've got a good touch," Dr. Janssen said as Wes returned.

Wes nodded in acknowledgement. He couldn't rope very well, but his affinity with animals was probably why a ranch job always seemed easy to get. He turned back to Steve. "Call me if you need help again—I can usually be here in ten or fifteen minutes."

"Thanks, Wes. Not sure what I would have done without you coming in."

"Anytime. See you tomorrow." Wes headed for his truck, but stopped as a small red Nissan pulled in.

Ellie.

The back passenger door opened, and Olivia swooshed out at a run. "Did you come to see my pony, Wes?"

Her slight lisp was adorable, and he smiled as he crouched to her level. "Actually, I didn't even know you had a pony." He didn't look up, but felt Ellie standing close.

"Her name's Daisy and she's a palomino and I love her!" Olivia announced. She grabbed his hand and pulled. "Come on!"

Ellie put a hand on her daughter's shoulder. "Honey, maybe Wes is going home. He's been driving the sleigh all day."

Olivia's smile disappeared. Her shoulders sagged, and Wes was surprised at the

tug on his heart.

"I think I've seen your palomino pony," he said, "but I would appreciate meeting her properly." He gave Ellie a helpless smile. "I didn't expect to see you guys out here," he said as Olivia dropped his hand and dashed ahead.

"She didn't want to leave her friends in New York, but the promise of a pony made a good bribe. And when you have an uncle with a stable…"

Ellie matched Wes's stride, but she was a good six feet away. That felt five feet too far for him. He still felt the connection they'd had in high school, no matter how much time had gone by.

She obviously didn't feel it, though. He was water under the bridge; his river had moved him far downstream from her years ago. Too far to ever get back.

At least she was speaking to him now.

⁂

ELLIE SMOOTHED COLOR ONTO MRS. COLLINS' hair, rolled it up, then did another. Not totally mindless, but familiar and automatic. Mrs. Collins liked to drift away in her thoughts, not talk, so Ellie's mind had room to roam, too.

Olivia had been so proud to introduce Daisy to Wes. She had chattered on about riding in the arena and on the trail, and proudly showed him that she could lift Daisy's hoof properly to pick it out.

Wes had smiled and listened attentively, asking questions that Olivia answered with long explanations. The whole time, he had kept glancing at Ellie like he couldn't keep his eyes off her.

She shivered as she remembered. She'd been so aware of his presence, his closeness, that it had been all she could do to stay two steps away from him. She wasn't at all sure how she felt about that.

She might be glad they had met again, glad to see how he'd grown into a man, and glad he was kind to her daughter.

But she wasn't sure that gladness carried over to finding out that she was still attracted to him, despite all the years that had passed.

And she was definitely not glad that attraction was worming its way into her heart.

He was only here to clear out his grandmother's house.

Taking over the sleigh rides for Uncle Steve was a generous thing to do, and Ellie was grateful for it, but it also meant that it would take Wes longer to finish his task.

Longer that she had to hide the return of her feelings.

Longer for her to imagine sliding back into his arms, into his kisses. Sharing secrets again, feeling one with someone again, going—

"Do you still have magazines at the back table?" Mrs. Collins asked.

Ellie came back to the present with a start, shocked to realize she had colored her client's whole head already. "Yes, of course." She helped Mrs. Collins out of the chair and settled her in the waiting area. "It will be about thirty minutes, maybe forty."

Ellie returned to her station to tidy up.

"Been dreaming of Cowboy Wes?" Merry joked.

The problem with being red-headed and fair-skinned was the ease with which a fiery-red blush crept up Ellie's face. "Not at all," she protested, gathering the bowl, brushes, and extra foils.

"Right." Merry smirked. "Keep saying that, and you might believe it someday. Except," her face became serious, "don't forget he's only here for a couple of weeks."

Ellie half-stomped to the supply area, but Merry was right. She determined to put Wes out of her mind. Since he would be heading back to his precious ranch, a short fling was all it could be. And since that was the last thing she wanted, she had to work harder to protect herself. The next time she let her mind wander, she'd focus on how she would design her own salon. If she ever found a place to rent.

Two shampoo-and-cuts and another color job later, Ellie was cleaning up when Merry pulled her to the side. "Alice was in the lobby impressing clients and gave me a paper to put in her office. You know what was up on her computer?" Merry's eyes gleamed mischievously.

Ellie raised her eyebrows.

"Alice is leaving!"

"Right," Ellie said. "And I've just won a million dollars."

"No joke. She had a confirmation letter onscreen—she starts managing a salon in San Francisco in mid-January."

Ellie gasped. "She's leaving? What will happen to the salon here? To us?"

"I was thinking…what's the possibility that the help wanted ad we saw was for La Chevelure?"

Ellie thudded into her styling chair. "Do you really think that was about us?" she squeaked. "We'll be getting a manager?"

"I'm not sure," Merry said, getting serious. "That copy of the *News* was two months old, so if she hasn't found someone by now…"

Ellie's mind worked furiously. Maybe she didn't have to start her own business from scratch. Maybe she could be Alice's manager. In New York, Marshall hadn't wanted her working, but he had no problem having a wife who was taking business classes, so she had a bit of training, just not the experience. Would that be enough for Alice?

"No," Merry said, crossing her arms.

"What?"

"You are NOT going to apply for the manager job."

"How did you…"

"Girlfriend, everything you think crosses your face. And no way do you want to tie yourself so closely with Alice."

She was right. Ellie shuddered at the thought of reporting sales and expenses to Alice, in addition to the pressure of increasing their clientele with just the right people. "So. someone else will come in and manage us."

Merry shrugged. "If she gets someone. If not…"

"If not, the salon will close," Ellie finished. She was silent a moment. "Unless…"

Merry encouraged, "Keep going."

Ellie took a deep breath. "Unless someone purchases the salon. Like me."

"Now you're getting there!"

Ellie wasn't sure whether to jump with excitement or collapse from the shock. "You think a lot bigger than me."

"Somebody has to." Merry's smile widened into a grin. "You've got a lot of figuring out to do. But better you than me!"

Merry turned back to her own station. The busy salon sounds re-entered Ellie's consciousness, and she checked her watch. Her next client wasn't due for another ten minutes, so she gave her station an extra cleaning and arranged her drawers and counter until they would make an OCD stylist proud. She had to do something while her mind whirled.

THAT NIGHT, Ellie listened to Olivia laugh watching *Moana* yet again, then turned back to her sister. "So I've written down some basic information, but not really enough for a proper business plan."

Abby looked at Ellie's paper and grimaced. "You don't know the cost of the lease or the utilities. You don't know what supplies cost. You don't know what taxes are. What *do* you know?"

"It's not that bad," Ellie protested. "I know the stylists will probably all stay, and their clients with them. And I do know that Alice makes good money on the shop, so it has to be earning enough to pay the lease and utilities and insurance and everything."

"Unless she's cutting corners," Abby said under her breath. "Do you guys pay for your own shampoo and such?"

Ellie shook her head. "We all use the salon's product lines so clients get a consistent result. I'll need to find out average costs for that, too."

It's a big risk," Abby warned. "It's even more of a risk if you don't know the basic info."

"I know," Ellie said. "But Abby, from the time I started cosmetology school, I wanted to run my own place. I thought when I eventually got the chance, it would be small. I never dreamed it could be La Chevelure itself."

Abby ran a finger around the rim of her coffee cup. "Do you have to buy the best salon in town, at what is sure to be a high price? Couldn't you start small like you planned?"

Ellie shook her head. "Starting small is all I could ever consider, and it would mean years of struggling to get a clientele. If Merry is willing to help with the cost…"

"Have you guys actually talked money yet? How much is she contributing, and can you match it?"

Ellie leaned back with a heavy sigh. "I know she's got way more than I can match, but I figure I'll be putting in the sweat equity and signing my name on the bank loan. I just wish I had the details I need."

Abby pursed her mouth, thinking.

"Mommy, Moana sailed home and saved her island and everyone!"

"Wasn't that great, sweetie? Can you go color for a while so I can talk to Aunt Abby?"

"Can I sing my song first?"

Ellie rolled her eyes, but Abby said, "Sure."

Olivia started with the chorus and danced while she sang, "All I want for Christmas is my two front teeth…" She forgot the second line of the verse, but segued smoothly into "Santa

Claus is Coming to Town." She finished with a flamboyant curtsey, then ran off to her coloring books.

Ellie turned back to her sister.

"You need to meet with Alice," Abby said, "If she's interested in selling, she'll have to give you all her details. You'd be buying the whole business, after all, not just taking over her lease."

"What if I can't afford it? Should I even approach her without knowing?"

Abby shrugged. "Talk to Merry and find out how much she wants to invest. Then talk to Ms. Lucas at the bank, explain everything, and see if they'll consider it. Contingent on meeting all their requirements, of course."

Ellie shook her head. "When did you get so wise?"

"Not wise, just protective of my little sister."

6

W es slapped the reins lightly across Sadie's haunches. The mare leaned into the harness and pulled the sleigh steadily forward.

It was their sixth trip that day, and Wes was bored out of his mind. There were only so many times a guy could look at the same Advent windows, point out the same carousel, drive past the same yappy white dog. He'd rather be cleaning out Grandma's attic, or better yet, be back on the ranch taking hay out to the cattle. Even mucking out stalls in Steve's barn would be better than this.

Sadie plodded on, and the three sisters taking their ride argued over which celebrities they'd seen in the shops. Wes tuned them out and let his thoughts wander back to holding the gelding for Dr. Janssen. He wouldn't want any other animals hurt, but he'd like to work with the vet again. Hold a horse, fetch a bandage, whatever. It felt good doing that, tending wounds, keeping animals healthy.

Ah, well, he was a rancher and he'd get back to it soon. Kuda and Sadie would have to be his animal fix until then.

In the meantime, there was a lot more to go through at Grandma's than he'd expected: more furniture in the attic, more boxes of papers. He wasn't even close to starting the painting, although he had patched a hole in the wall where the doorknob kept hitting. He ought to be back there now, not driving a sleigh for grumpy tourists. If he were, he might actually get done by Christmas.

On the other hand, the papers would drive him stir-crazy if he didn't get out in the fresh air enough. And working with Sadie, scratching her ears while they waited for the next customers, offering her handfuls of grain, also kept him sane. Taking her back to the stable made him want to hang around, not rush back to Grandma's boxes.

Besides, Ellie might bring Olivia out to ride the pony.

Ellie, with her sassy hair and kissable mouth. Ellie, who still held a place in his heart after all these years. Ellie, whom he'd like to whisk away for a romantic dinner and gaze into those green eyes all evening long.

Man, he had it bad.

He'd tried to convince himself he wanted their friendship back, but finally admitted that nine years on, he still wasn't over her. She'd made it plenty clear she was over him, though. Wanted nothing to do with him romantically, and he didn't think he could handle being "just friends."

The thought of quitting the sleigh rides and rushing through the work at Grandma's house crossed his mind, but he couldn't go back on his word to Steve.

Back at his marked-off parking spot next to the town square, he helped the sisters down from the sleigh. The brunette never stopped talking. "I don't see how you could miss her! Thanks, Wes. I swear it was Gretchen Blaise herself! When she…"

As soon as they left, Wes's eyes went to Ellie's salon.

There had to be a way he could entice her on a date. And if not, he ought to just junk all Grandma's stuff and head back to Black Rock Ranch. No, more than that. He'd go home and hang up his hat, as far as women were concerned anyway.

He turned back to Kuda and motioned permission to get down from the seat. Kuda hopped to the ground, rolled in the snow, then moved forward to sniff Sadie. The mare lowered her head to sniff him back, and Wes smiled. These were the parts of his life he loved.

He grabbed a rag and rubbed the one or two spots where Sadie had begun to sweat.

Suddenly Ellie's voice rang out from across the street. "Wes!" She stopped for a break in traffic, then hurried over to him. "Wes, Uncle Steve needs you at the barn. Can you come? I can put Sadie away." She began fumbling with the harness buckles.

"Is he hurt again?" He nudged her aside—evidently she could saddle a horse but not unharness one—and swiftly unhitched the mare.

"I guess. I only talked to him on the phone, but he's done something bad to his leg." She looked at the harness. "And thanks, I would have had it unbuckled into all its little pieces."

Wes looped the long reins over his arm, undid a few straps, and lifted the hefty collar off Sadie's withers. He dumped it all in the sleigh, then slipped the mare's bridle off, snapping a lead rope on her halter. "Is he at the hospital?"

"Not yet. Won't go until you get there, stubborn man." Ellie frowned and led Sadie to the trailer.

Wes scooped up the harness and left the sleigh where it was. They loaded Sadie quickly, and Kuda jumped into the truck before Wes climbed in. "I'll keep you posted."

She nodded, relief showing in her face.

Wes arrived at the stables in near record time, as much as he could pulling a live load. The riding instructor was sitting with Steve on some hay bales, while another woman paced the aisle talking on the phone and a third was holding two horses in the arena.

"Wes, good," Steve said through clenched teeth. "My evening helper quit today, and I figured I'd start bringing the horses in. Got caught between the old gray gelding and a fence post."

Wes looked at Steve's leg, the cast smeared with dust and dirt marks now. Steve had both hands wrapped around his thigh above it, and the woman had her hand on his shoulder. Wes could see he was barely keeping things together. "What do you need me to do? Drive you to the hospital?"

Steve shook his head. "The horses. Shayla here knows them well enough to get them into their stalls. She just can't stay to feed." He pulled a sharp breath and paused, closing his eyes before he continued. "Instructions are on the whiteboard above the grain barrels. About half of them get supplements, and those are listed too. If you could take care of that, I can get this leg looked at again."

Wes helped Steve to his feet, and with Shayla on his good side and Wes on his bad, they helped Steve hop out to a blue SUV. His face paled as they settled him on the seat.

The woman on the phone appeared and went to the driver's side. "They're expecting him. Call and let me know what they say."

"I'll be back tonight," Steve insisted. But his eyes were closed, and his face was still tense with pain. Wes didn't think he'd be home anytime soon.

He watched the SUV until it turned down the main road,

then followed Shayla back into the barn. She and the other rider put the two saddled horses into their stalls.

"That'll keep the aisle clear to bring the others in. Mary will take care of them both," Shayla said, striding confidently to the outer barn door.

Together they sorted the horses into their stalls. Wes thanked Shayla, Mary departed with her, and he was left alone in the barn. Fine with him—that was how he liked it.

Before he went to the feed room, Wes went into the stalls and ran his hands over each horse, checking for cuts and scrapes and unexpected heat. Now would not be the time to have an injured horse on top of an injured barn owner.

He wondered what Steve had done to his leg. Broken it again? Hurt something above or below the cast? The man shouldn't have been out here anyway. He should have called Wes. Or Ellie. Ellie could have brought the horses in with Steve directing her.

Wes smiled at the thought of Ellie doing ranch work. She was petite, but determined—he was sure she'd be bossing everyone else's horses around in no time. He wondered what he could do to convince her to boss him around.

"Wes? Are you here?"

Wes straightened at the sound of Ellie's voice, chuckling that his thoughts could make her appear. "Over here," he called. He gave the black horse a last pat on the shoulder and latched the stall carefully behind him.

"I came as soon as I could. I finally got a hold of Mom— she's meeting Uncle Steve at the hospital—and Abby is picking Olivia up. How's Steve?"

Wes tore himself away from admiring her freckles. "Not great. In a lot of pain, holding on through sheer force of will."

Ellie groaned. "What happened?"

Wes shook his head. "He lost his evening help and

decided he could bring the horses in on his own. Didn't work out too well."

Ellie pulled her shoulders back and stood tall. "What can I do now?"

"I was checking the horses first, haven't started feeding yet." A whinny across the barn echoed his words. Wes smiled. "As you can tell."

Ellie grinned, sending his thoughts far away from the horses. He'd give anything to lean down and kiss her right now, but he'd probably get slapped for his efforts.

"So let's go feed," she said, striding confidently to the feed room.

"Have you done this before?" he asked, his long legs quickly catching up.

"Not since I was a kid. I've only gone in to get a handful of grain for Daisy when Olivia was done riding."

Together, they scooped oats and sweet feed, added vitamins and other supplements, and delivered the buckets to hungry horses. Wes gave each a pat and quick check as he poured their grain while Ellie took the empty bucket back and wheeled the cart to the next stall.

Then it was back to load a bale of alfalfa in the cart, dropping a flake off for each horse. They finished at Daisy's stall, a small one tucked in the corner because she didn't need as much room. She didn't get as much hay, either.

"Poor Daisy," Ellie said, scratching her withers as she gobbled a mouthful. "No grain, only a bit of hay. Steve says she'll founder, otherwise."

Wes nodded. "Ponies don't do well on a lot of rich food. Don't need it either, not like a horse in heavy work."

Ellie looked up at him. "You really like this, don't you?"

"Don't know what I'd do if I didn't have a horse in my

life. Being cooped up at Grandma's would drive me crazy without this."

"You're already crazy," Ellie teased. "Have been since you were a kid."

"True, but it takes one to know one."

"Oh, we're back in high school now?"

Wes smiled, wishing that were true. If it were, he'd pour his heart out to her and then pull her in for a kiss. As it was, he had to be satisfied with her just being in the barn at the same time as him. And joking! Joking was good.

"Hey, Wes," Ellie said. "Are you only into horses and cattle these days? Or do you still ski?"

Wes snorted. "The only skis I've been on lately have been the ones on the snowmobile, checking on the herd in the winter."

"Oh really?" Her eyes held a challenge. "Then you wouldn't be interested in a downhill run or two?"

"Says you. Just try me."

"Except...what about the sleigh rides?"

He sighed. He just plain old had too many commitments. "I haven't had a day off since I took them over."

"Surely Sadie needs a rest day, too?" Ellie rested her hand on Daisy's neck. Her face looked thoughtful, and Wes watched her smooth strands of Daisy's coarse mane. She started to speak a few times, only to close her mouth again.

Finally she said, "Could you manage a Sunday? I'm working Saturday, but suppose you let people know the sleigh rides will be closed Sunday, and we go skiing instead?"

Skiing with Ellie again. Anticipation surged faster than a cutting horse after a steer. Fun and laughter and excitement and fresh air. Maybe they'd land in the snow together. Friendship, and maybe more.

No, she was the one who had said "just friends," and he

needed to respect that. But this was softening, wasn't it? Maybe sometime soon she'd give him some signals she might want more.

Wes nodded, keeping the possibilities tamped down inside him. "Sounds good," was all he said.

7

Ellie shampooed her young client's hair absentmindedly, her thoughts still out at the stable from the night before. She'd been thinking how much she missed Wes's friendship and had had a sudden idea. She'd tried to think it through logically, but his closeness had kept her mind muddled until she'd blurted it out.

An invitation to go skiing.

Now, clear-headed and more sensible, she wondered if she'd ever been more stupid. She wasn't a robot—did she really think she could handle being "just friends" with Wes? That she could keep her head in charge, locking away the feelings that rose every time she saw him?

"...pastel colors," Mindy was saying.

"I'm sorry," Ellie replied, mortified at her mental disappearance. "I didn't catch that."

"I want my colors to be more pastel than super-bright," the teenager said. "Can you do that?"

"Of course. I've got a gorgeous powder pink that you'll love." Ellie sent Mindy back to the styling chair with her hair wrapped in a towel and went to get the rainbow colors she'd asked for.

Alice's office door was open, and she caught some of the words. *...not much luck finding a manager...I'll be there in... might have to sell...wouldn't change...*

Ellie took extra time finding the four shades until Alice's conversation ended. With her hands full, she knocked on Alice's doorway.

Alice looked up, her face strained. "Yes?"

"I'm sorry, but your door was open, and I couldn't help but overhear," Ellie began. "You're thinking of selling?"

Alice pursed her lips. "It's not common knowledge, but yes, maybe."

Ellie stood there, not sure what to say next.

"Don't worry, I'm sure your job is safe."

"I...thank you, but...I'm interested in buying," Ellie blurted out.

Alice's eyes almost bugged out. "You?"

Ellie nodded. "Me and Merry together."

"But...you're recently divorced and she's widowed and you're both single parents."

Ellie gave a half-smile. "Our finances aren't common knowledge, either. But we've been talking about possibilities and we might be interested. If you're serious about selling, I'd like some details."

Alice pursed her lips. "I had hoped to find a manager to take over, but the ones I've interviewed aren't...suitable." She glanced at her desk calendar and frowned. "I have a deadline, however. Perhaps..." She tapped her lips and then nodded decisively. "I'll let you know when I've talked to my accountant."

Ellie was almost dancing as she headed back to her client's soon-to-be-colorful hair.

. . .

ELLIE GRINNED the next day as Wes took three tries to snap his ski boots into his skis. "Haven't kept up the skiing during your cowboy days, huh?"

Wes looked up, frowning. "Not much time off the ranch, even in winter."

"That's all right. We'll start you back on the bunny slopes." She knew there was a wicked gleam in her eyes, but she wasn't going to tell him that Olivia always started there anyway.

She and Olivia swooshed over to the chair lift line. Wes followed with careful strides.

"I was scared the first time, too," Olivia reassured him. "Just wait for it and you won't fall down."

"Thank you, I'll remember that," he said. "Do you have any advice for getting off?"

"Get out of the way of the next person!" Olivia shouted.

Wes laughed. "Sounds like the voice of experience."

Ellie loved the way he connected with her daughter. He didn't talk down to her and seemed to appreciate her for herself, not just a tag-along.

Wes followed them up the slope, with Olivia turning around and waving several times. Ellie had to remind the six-year-old several times to sit still and be ready to get off. They disembarked smoothly and watched Wes.

Wes landed easily and glided over to them, his long, lean body just as easy on skis as she remembered. Memories of past ski days washed over her: racing down the slopes, falling and picking each other up when they tried an unfamiliar run, his face red with wind and exertion, his eyes dancing with the fun.

Would it be so bad to see if there was something still

there? He was obviously willing, but could she risk her heart again?

She reminded herself that he was going back to the ranch, probably before Christmas. She really did need to keep things at a friendship level.

"Shall we go?" Ellie said, adjusting her pole in her hands. "You lead off, Olivia."

She had brought Olivia back to Huckleberry Falls in mid-spring, with two months left in the ski season, and her daughter had shown herself to be a natural on skis. They had only been once or twice this season, but Olivia had mastered the beginner slopes already. She still liked to start on the bunny slope, though—it was an easy glide to get her warmed up and ready to concentrate.

Olivia looked at Ellie with a gap-toothed grin and set off down the hill.

Wes looked at Ellie with a gleaming grin and pushed off after her.

Ellie watched them with a happy-go-lucky grin, then followed.

They spent the morning up and down chair lifts, from the bunny slope to the two green-circle beginner runs, smiling and swooshing and showing off.

Well, Wes tried to show off, anyway.

As a teenager, he had played with jumps and spins, and Ellie had always enjoyed watching him. As an adult nearly ten years later, she still enjoyed it, but for different reasons.

He tried to do a wide split in the air, but he landed on one ski before the other and wobbled comically for quite a while before he steadied.

When he tried to do a full 360 in the air, though, he only made it half way around and flailed wildly as he skied backward unexpectedly. Rather like a cartoon character, Ellie thought, laughing.

His backward run lasted about fifteen feet before he tumbled over a few times, and her laughs turned to gasps as she rushed toward him.

"Wes! Are you okay?"

He lay motionless, then opened his eyes and blinked. "I guess my skills need a little brushing up."

"You think?" She reached a hand down to help him up.

He shook off the snow and kept a hand on her shoulder while he worked the kinks out of his legs. The pressure was warm and comforting and...

It wasn't a decade earlier, though. Ellie scanned the slope and found Olivia's pink ski suit at the bottom. Good.

She didn't doubt Olivia's abilities at this level, but Wes's antics had made her forget her responsibilities for a few minutes. And that was not good.

"Come, on," Ellie said. "Olivia's waiting at the bottom, and I think it's time for a lunch break."

ELLIE WRAPPED her hands around her mug of hot chocolate, sighed with the warm comfort, and then slurped some of the whipped cream on top.

Olivia giggled. "Mommy, you look like Mr. Baxter!"

Wes raised his eyebrows. "Old Bluffing Baxter? He's still around?"

Ellie nodded. "And his mustache is whiter and bushier than ever."

"It wiggles when he reads us stories at the library." The six-year-old wiggled her lip with her finger in imitation.

Wes stirred his melting whipped cream into his chocolate. "Not teaching science anymore, huh? He got me excited about biology and the way all a body's systems worked together, said I had an intuitive understanding about it."

Ellie looked at him. "You weren't too excited about school though, were you? You'd spend your extra time drawing instead of getting your homework done early."

"That's me, Mr. Procrastinator." Wes leaned back in his seat and frowned.

"Mr. Pro-tator?" Olivia puzzled through the word. "I thought you were Mr. Wes."

Ellie leaned into her daughter. "He is Mr. Wes, honey. A *pro-cras-tin-ator* is someone who puts off doing something until it's too late."

"Hey!" Wes protested. "I still got my assignments turned in on time!"

"Yeah, by staying up half the night." Ellie smirked.

"Well, *some* of us liked to have fun while we could." He waggled his eyebrows.

Olivia giggled again, and the two of them made faces at each other while Ellie let herself remember.

Sometimes she had spent hours working on an essay while Wes was off with his buddies, shooting cans up in the hills. They rode horses often, sometimes having laughter-filled trotting races down the dirt road along Uncle Steve's hay field. Sometimes they had "studied" together, Wes drawing doodles on her left arm while she wrote math problems with her right. Of course, that was followed with her playing with his hair while he tried to concentrate on Macbeth.

He may have procrastinated, but he had been good at finishing things eventually.

Was his wanderlust part of his procrastination? When he'd left after high school, she thought he'd be gone forever, that he'd never want to settle down.

Wes seemed different, now, though. More mature, and not just in years. Still fun-loving, but more responsible.

It was obvious he wanted to pick up their relationship, and it was becoming equally obvious to Ellie that she was still half in love with him. More than she wanted to admit. "Just friends" didn't seem to be where her heart was.

Could it be worth the risk? Or were these just excuses to indulge herself in a bit of love, and then she'd get her heart broken all over again?

Ellie took a few sips of hot chocolate and let the soothing liquid slide down her throat and warm her throughout. "So tell me about this ranch you're working on."

Wes made one more funny face for Olivia, then leaned back with his mug. "It's actually pretty great. It's called Black Rock Ranch, and it's owned by three brothers. Well, four actually, but one is off in Iraq. We've got about four hundred head of cattle and—"

"Do you lasso them?" Olivia burst in.

Wes gave her a sheepish grin. "I'm actually the worst cowboy for roping that they've ever had. No matter how much I practice, that lasso keeps tangling on me. Or twisting in the air. Or landing on the stump next to the one I'm aiming for."

Ellie laughed. "And they still keep you around?"

"I may be the worst at roping, but Adam says I'm one of the best for working with the young horses and injured animals." He blushed lightly as he spoke, and Ellie's heart thumped a little faster.

"So do modern ranchers go on cattle drives and everything?" she asked.

Wes's lips quirked. "And everything. We take most of the herd up to summer pastures and bring them down again. We feed them in the winter, pull calves in the spring, fix fences and tractors and everything else that breaks down."

Ellie pictured him working outdoors all year. "Is the snow down there awful?"

He shrugged, and Ellie enjoyed watching his changing expressions. "Unless we get a blizzard that hits too fast for the cows to find shelter, the snow's just something to live with. It's the mud in the spring that's awful. It covers *everything*."

"Even your head?" Olivia giggled and squirmed.

"Now you're just being silly," Ellie told her. "Are you getting too wound up?"

Olivia quieted immediately. "No, Mommy. We don't need to go home."

Ellie pushed the restaurant's crayons and coloring page to her while Wes studied his napkin. "Here, you'll like this."

Olivia sighed heavily, and Wes quirked a smile again. After a moment of coloring, Olivia asked, "Do you have a horse? Is his name Sparky?"

"Sparky?"

"Sheriff Callie's horse," Ellie explained. "It's a kid's cartoon from a few years back. Olivia's been bingeing it lately."

"I don't binge, Mommy," the girl protested. "You only let me watch two a day."

"That's because you only get an hour of TV a day, kiddo. You'd watch more if you could."

"So, tell me about being a hair stylist or beautician or whatever you call it," Wes said brightly.

It was a nice chance of subject, but... "I cut hair. What else is there to tell?"

"What do you like best about it?"

"Making people look good, I guess. No," she corrected herself, "it's seeing the light in their face and the way they walk out when *they* know they look good. I guess I like boosting people's confidence."

"Um-hmm," Wes murmured, his eyes locked with hers. "What do you *not* like about it?"

Ellie huffed. "That's easy—my boss!"

His eyebrows raised in a silent question.

"She's a tyrant. She bends over backwards for prominent people, toadies up to them, and doesn't mind hurting regular folks while she does it. It's all about the bottom line —she made Merry and me work late suddenly one night, expecting us to instantly find family to take care of the kids."

"Ooh boy," Wes said. "A bad boss can make a job miserable."

"Speaking from experience? How did you solve the problem?"

He snorted. "I left. There's always another ranch out there." He studied her face. "How many other salons are in town?"

"A few, but none I could move to. But…" She clenched her hands. Could she talk about what might only be a dream?

She looked straight into Wes's brown eyes, seeing only encouragement. "I may have heard that my boss is leaving. And I may be making an offer to buy the salon."

If they had been in a cartoon, his jaw would have unhinged and dropped all the way to the floor, and his eyes would be bugged out across the room. As it was, well, she hadn't caught Wes Colton speechless too many times before.

"Yeah," she said with a smile, "that's about how I feel."

"Wow, so you're going to be the evil boss lady?"

"A *nice* boss lady, I hope."

"But…how are you managing to *buy* a salon?" His eyes were dark with concern now. "I mean, I don't imagine cutting hair gives you a six-figure income, and you're a single mom. Or did you take your ex to the cleaners?"

Ellie huffed. "I got decent child support but nothing else. My lawyer's still trying to get a settlement for me. But I've saved some, and I can get a bank loan."

"Still…"

"And remember Merry Hurst? She's going to be my behind-the-scenes partner. She wants to invest Ray's life insurance, so my bank loan will be half the total price."

Wes reached across the table and took her hand. A familiar heart-rushing feeling ran through her. "I'm excited for you—you can do this."

The look on his face, the way her senses were heightened, the feeling that he was on her side and would do anything to help… It was like the last nine years had never happened. They had each other's backs, not to mention their hearts.

She dragged her focus back to the conversation. "If it all goes through. I need a lot more details before I can even do a business plan." Numbers and calculations were hard to think of now, though, as the warmth from Wes's touch spread through her body. It reminded her of soft summer nights, holding hands and talking under the stars. Or cuddling on the couch while they watched a movie. All the ways things used to be and could be again.

Her thoughts must have transmitted. Wes looked at their hands, then back to her eyes. He smiled, that soft, wondrous smile that had always melted her heart.

Would he lean across and kiss her like he used to? Did she want him to?

"Mommy, are we going to ski some more?"

Ellie sucked in a breath. Right. Like she should be kissing someone in front of her six-year-old daughter.

She pulled her hand away from Wes's. "Yes, we are. Thank

you for the reminder." She fumbled the silverware as she tidied the table.

Wes gathered the napkins and added them to a plate, his hand brushing against her fingers.

She jerked her hand away, a mish-mash of feelings tumbling through her. "Do you want to keep your coloring page?" she asked Olivia.

Olivia shook her head and scooted her chair back. "It would just get smushed skiing."

"Right you are," Wes said. "So if you're not burdened with a coloring page, what run are you going to race me down next?"

Olivia made a face at him. "We don't need to race—I beat you to the bottom every time anyway."

"Maybe I'll be faster if I pretend I'm on a horse."

Olivia looked doubtful, and Ellie laughed. "You're doing really well today, Olivia. Want to try an intermediate run? We can see how rusty Wes's show-off skills really are.

"Yes!" Olivia shouted.

"You're on," Wes said.

Ellie caught the glimmer in his eyes and knew her own reflected it. And she had to admit it wasn't all about the skiing.

8

The skiing was only a delightful memory by the next morning. Wes gritted his teeth and glared at three more boxes in Grandma's bedroom. Where had they come from, and would they ever end? He'd much rather be out in the fresh air, preferably back on skis or on a horse. Even taking silly tourists around in the sleigh would be better.

A memory came full force, as if he were still there: he was maybe seven years old, and his mother sat across the dining table. He was staring at the small pile of peas next to his mashed potatoes, hating the green sight of them.

"Sometimes it's easier to do the hard stuff first and get it over with," his mother had said. "That way you can enjoy the rest of your meal." She nodded encouragingly.

He took a deep breath and bravely ate the first disgusting bite. He forced himself to swallow and shoved the second bite in. Only two peas left now, and he scooped them up with some mashed potatoes. Done!

"Doesn't that feel better now?" his mother asked. It didn't, really, but he liked having pleased her. And he did like eating his chicken and potatoes without having the peas staring at him.

Wes chuckled now. He still wasn't thrilled to eat peas, but he'd learned well to tackle the hard stuff just to get it out of the way. These three boxes were definitely hard stuff, but once he was done, there shouldn't be any more. He hoped.

He plunked the first one on the bed, blew the dust off the top, and opened it up.

Pictures. Loads and loads of pictures from his non-digital grandmother.

Didn't grandmas have plenty of time to put pictures into albums? How was he supposed to know which ones to keep?

The first photos were recent ones of his dad. Most were just Dad at a barbecue or Christmas or something, with Bombshell Barbie only appearing in a few. One had him asleep on the couch with Grandma's cat curled up beside him.

Wes smiled at the sight, but it made his heart contract. When Dad had married Barbara, Wes had started spending more time at Grandma's than at home until finally he'd moved all his belongings over permanently. Barbie was shrill and judgmental, with no patience for teenage boys. Dad, newly in love and trying to keep peace at home, usually took Barbie's side. When Wes had left after graduation, there didn't seem to be much reason to keep in touch.

Dad had finally seen through his manipulative new wife and divorced her a couple years ago, but the relationship damage had been done. Other than joint tears at Grandma's funeral, they often seemed more like acquaintances than father and son.

Now, Wes missed both his parents. Mom was gone, and the grief would always be there, but Dad was still here. Well, not *here*, but around. After the divorce, he had taken an oil rig job overseas and seemed to be hopping from place to place even more than Wes.

Huh. New thought to consider: maybe Wes's itchy feet were inherited, not just a character flaw.

He saved the picture of Dad asleep with the cat, but tossed the rest into a trash box. He flipped through more that didn't mean anything to him—some of Grandma's friends, he supposed, and places she had visited.

Then he stopped short.

A photo of him and Ellie stared up from the pile. They were on the porch, his arms around her, with her sassy red hair flying into his face. Both of them were laughing, and the picture radiated joy.

Wes picked it up and just looked. They had been so perfect together. Friendship, love, doing everything together as if they were joined at the hip.

Eagerly, he pulled more photos from the box. The time they'd had a pie eating contest at Grandma's counter, faces smeared with blackberry filling; the two of them returning from a trail ride, sweaty and tired, but still smiling; the ever-present Monopoly game, with Wes and Ellie locking eyes in a stare-down over Boardwalk.

He had loved her so much. Why had he ever let her go?

Because he hadn't wanted to be tied to Huckleberry Falls forever, and she'd wanted to stay.

Because he'd wanted to make it on his own.

Because he'd wanted to see more of the world.

Because—Wes caught his breath—he'd been afraid.

The realization had him sinking to the floor, photos clutched in his hands. It had never crossed his mind before, but there was truth in it. He slowed his thoughts down and considered. Afraid of what?

Not Ellie herself. She'd been all that was good in his life.

Well, besides Grandma.

Had he been afraid of marrying her because she'd been the only girlfriend he'd ever had? Because he was leery of falling into something just because it was expected?

Wes flipped through the pictures again and shook his head. They might have been teenagers, but their love had been solid. Ellie hadn't gone so far as to plan their wedding, but she'd talked of the house she'd like to have, how she would decorate it.

Had he been afraid of commitment because he was so young? Afraid of making the wrong choice like his father had? Perhaps he'd been running from his father's disastrous marriage as much as anything. Ellie had suggested just that before he'd left, but he'd shrugged her off.

He had come to his senses finally, at least a little. He didn't move around as much now, and Black Rock Ranch had become home. But when he had visited Grandma after that first year or two, Ellie was gone to New York, married to some guy who'd swept her off her feet.

He sighed. Whatever the reason, he'd goofed up and lost her. But that was then. Now he was back, and she was back, and he suddenly knew he wanted more than a couple of dates with Ellie.

He wanted *her*. In his arms. In his life. Forever.

Wes just had to figure out how to make that work.

Oh, and convince her, too.

ELLIE WORKED THROUGH THE DAY, checking out the window for Wes and the sleigh every time she met a client out front. She smiled when she saw him and walked back a little slower when he wasn't there.

Now, she finished sweeping up after her evening client, hanks of long dark hair filling the dust pan. She hoped Maria would be happy with her new, short bob. She checked in at the desk to see if anyone else had been scheduled late, then caught another glimpse of Wes out the front window.

He stood talking to Bart Williams from the B&B. The streetlight shone down on them, and the way he tilted his head whisked her back to a decade earlier. He'd looked just that way when they were planning an escapade that her parents might not like. She didn't know what he was planning now, but it was surely something.

Mr. Williams left, and Ellie scooted out the door. "Wes!"

He turned quickly, a smile flashing onto his face. "Hey, Ellie. You done with work?"

She eyed him speculatively. His eyes were dancing, his hair ruffling in the breeze. She had to find out what he was excited about. "Come on in," she said. "I need you for a few minutes."

He followed her back into the warmth, shedding his coat as they walked back to her station. "Have a seat," she directed.

He raised his eyebrows, but draped his coat over the chair next to them and obeyed.

She whisked out a drape and covered his clothes. "Don't you think it's time you got rid of that shaggy look?" She gave him a wicked grin.

Wes held up his hands and began to protest, then sank back in the chair. "You're right. I haven't had a haircut in...four or five months?"

"And it looks like it." Ellie picked up her spray bottle and began wetting his hair. "Time for a makeover, cowboy."

He shuddered as the cool water hit his neck, but then relaxed. "See, I told you. You *like* bossing people around."

"Only the people that need bossing," she shot back.

"Seems to me you're someone who needs it. Remember the time you wouldn't let me boss you? When you took the rope swing over the river in the spring, dropped in, and about turned into a block of ice?"

He gave a shiver and chuckled. "You don't forget a thing, do you?"

No, she didn't. She remembered when he'd dunked her into a water trough at Uncle Steve's, and when she'd stuffed a bandana inside his trumpet and he couldn't get a breath through it. She remembered the way she'd felt when they were together—happy, content, whole. And how empty she'd been when he left.

Her world had revolved around him back then. Not to the point that she was subsumed by him; it was more that they fit together perfectly, like they weren't complete without the other.

She'd felt those feelings coming back through the last week. Coming back way too quickly for her comfort, actually, but she had to admit the feelings were real. The question was, what did she want to do with them?

"So," she said, combing lightly, "the other day it sounded like you've really fallen in love with ranching."

Wes shrugged, keeping his head still. "I like it well enough, but I'm realizing it's more that I don't know what else to do, not that it's the dream job I always wanted."

Ellie already had her dream job and couldn't imagine doing anything else. Except owning the place herself. But if Wes was just marking time...the thought broke her heart.

"I asked yesterday," she said, checking the length on the sides, "but tell me again what you like best about it. More specifically than 'the horses.'"

Wes was quiet for a long moment, and Ellie moved behind him and combed through four inches of hair. She couldn't help but notice how broad his shoulders and upper back were. He was no gangly teenager anymore.

"I'd still have to say the horses. I like working with the youngsters," he said.

"The really young horses they breed, or training them, or what?"

He shrugged, then stilled as she tipped his head forward. "Training, I guess. I like gentling the colts, getting them calm and used to people. And starting them under saddle—I hate the term 'breaking.' I want a horse to be steady on his own, not because I've broken his spirit."

Ellie nodded. That sounded like her Wes. "So, what about becoming a horse trainer?"

He shook his head immediately. She huffed and used both hands to freeze his head in position again.

"You gotta be really involved with horse shows or rodeos and such to make a name for yourself. And there's a lot of politics involved. Definitely not for me."

"What else do you do that you like?" she asked.

At the same time, Wes said, "The other thing I really like is helping the vet when she comes."

Ellie giggled and bent toward his ear. "Is it the work or the vet you especially like?"

Wes snorted. "If you could see Dr. Sue, you'd know. I think she's older than my dad and just as dictatorial."

Hmm. That was a loaded statement if she had ever heard one. But this wasn't the time to go there. "So...vet work? Blood doesn't bother you?"

"Nope. Sometimes I'm heading the injured horse while Dr. Sue works, but if it's bad, someone else is there while I hold a leg so she can stitch and bandage. It's fascinating. Actually, so is the other stuff besides injuries. Did you know a horse's teeth get sharp edges and you have to file them off with a steel rasp? In fact, on the ranch I do a lot of the general maintenance with their health—give them shots, poultice a cut hoof, do the worming..."

Ellie had stopped snipping half way through and stared at him in silence. She'd never known Wes to be that excited about anything.

"What?" He turned around. "Are you done?"

She shook herself. "No, not at all." She went back to measuring and snipping. "You ever thought about being a vet yourself?"

"Hah! You know how many years of college that is?" He paused, then said, "Four years for my bachelor's and four more for vet school, right? I'd be thirty-eight by the time I finished. *If* I could manage to go full time."

Ellie took one last check on his sides and ran her comb through the back of his hair. What could she say to encourage him? He'd be a fantastic vet, and he was dismissing it out of hand.

She moved to the front and snipped one or two more places. "So if you *don't* go to vet school, where will you be in eight years?"

He snorted. "You think I should go to college with all the eighteen year olds? I'd rather spend my time on the ranch, thank you very much."

She let it go, sad for his future, but hoping that maybe she'd planted a seed. He deserved something he was passionate about.

Passionate.

They had had something passionate, and her heart told her they could have it again. But it took commitment to make the passion last. If he couldn't do it for a career he'd love, was he capable of doing it for her?

9

E llie's words echoed through Wes's mind as he took pictures down and filled nail holes early the next morning. What would it be like to be a vet instead of a ranch hand? Did he have that much ambition? And was that enough to carry him through eight years of college?

He suddenly dropped the putty knife and drove to Dr. Janssen's. The receptionist pointed him to the back parking lot, where the vet was getting his truck ready to go out on calls.

"Can I talk to you for a minute?" Wes asked after greeting him.

"Sure," Dr. Janssen said, pushing his cowboy hat back. "Grab that bucket of supplies there, will you?"

Wes took it to him and watched as the older man put gauze and medicines into particular places in his truck compartments. "What's it like doing this all day? Do you ever get tired of it?"

"Being a vet? All the time." Dr. Janssen laughed. "Sub-zero mornings, calls in the middle of the night, owners who could have prevented a nasty injury. But I wouldn't give it up, if that's what you're asking." He pointed to another plastic container.

Wes handed it to him, and the vet continued. "There is nothing like saving a cow that would have died, or seeing a horse running barrels again because you got his leg healed up properly. Or helping a mare having a difficult time foaling. Sure, there are hard cases, and sure, I'd like my sleep some nights, but I wouldn't trade it for the world." He peered at Wes. "Why're you asking?"

Wes scuffed the toe of his boot on the frosty asphalt. He kept his head down while he spoke. "Something somebody said. Made me think about vet school and if eight long years is worth it. I'm almost thirty as it is."

Dr. Janssen was quiet, and Wes finally looked up to see the man watching him. Wes shrugged. "Thanks for the chat. I'd better let you get to work."

Dr. Janssen eyed him a moment longer, then said, "Why don't you join me this morning? See what it's like out in the field."

Wes scuffed his boot some more. It was only eight o'clock now, and he'd planned to get the masking tape around Grandma's windows before the sleigh rides. "How long do you think you'll be out?"

The vet shrugged. "You never really know, but I've got three stops. Maybe two or three hours, unless one of them is really quick."

Grandma's paint prep could wait. And for that matter, the sleigh rides could wait a bit if they needed to. "Thanks, you've got a partner for the morning."

They climbed in the newly-stocked truck and headed out to a yearling colt who was listless and off his feed. Between the colt, who was running a temperature for which Dr.

Janssen took a blood sample, a check on a cow with a premature calf, and a horse with a hoof puncture, they talked about the seasons of veterinary work: foaling, calving, lambing; stress injuries from overwork; predator attacks in the long winter and early spring. About vet school: anatomy for multiple species, chemistry, pharmacology. And the cost.

"Your undergrad won't be too bad," Dr. Janssen said, "but if you want the grades to get into vet school, you'd better plan on a lot of work to ace your math and science classes instead of trying to hold down a job at the same time."

College classes and no paycheck. Was that even possible? "And vet school itself?" Wes asked, his body tight with tension.

Dr. Janssen chuckled. "Expensive. Ask me how I know."

Wes followed his lead. "How do you know?"

"Because my daughter is in her first year. And guess who's paying for it."

The truck hit a pothole, and Wes felt like all his hopes deflated with the jarring bounce. He'd never be able to afford it. "Is she going to be your partner?"

"No, she wants to get into research. Which means additional internship years, too." He sighed, then looked over at Wes. "Don't let the cost get you down. There are scholarships and student loans available. If you really want it, you'll find a way."

This had been the best morning Wes had had in a long time, but he had to be crazy. He was latching on to a dream he couldn't have. An immense cost, no job to earn money, and studying his brains out while the youngsters probably partied every weekend and still got good grades.

Those were very bleak-looking school years. Where would his hopes with Ellie fit in all of it? "It seems impossible," he finally said.

The vet was silent for a moment, then said, "How old are you again?"

"Almost thirty."

"And when you turn forty, if you're not a vet, what *will* you be?"

"Still ranching, probably." Wes gave a silent sigh.

"Do you like that future?"

Wes kept his mouth shut. There was altogether too much push and pull in his brain, and he was glad when they pulled back into the office parking lot. He thanked Dr. Janssen and said goodbye, looking forward to the simple task of grooming and harnessing Sadie.

ELLIE AND WES strolled through the crisp evening air, shoulders close but not quite touching. She looked up at him, still trying to reconcile this adult version of the boy she once knew. His skin was weather-rough, stubble shadowed his jaw, and the look in eyes had more force and determination than she remembered. Part of growing up, she supposed, and learning to work outdoors in all conditions, whether you liked it or not. She'd always thought of Wes as coasting through life, doing what he wanted instead of what he needed, but it didn't sound like an easy-going, care-free type of person would make it on a ranch.

They gazed into festive shop windows as they passed. "Ooh," Ellie said, pulling him into Torta al Cioccolato. "Have you been in here lately? I'm dying for one of their chocolate pastries."

"Still never pass up a chance for chocolate?" Wes's words cut off as he gazed at the display case.

Ellie joined him, nearly drooling at the fruit, chocolate or cream-filled pastries. Italian, but Swiss at the same time.

"You look like you need a little time," said someone from behind the counter.

Ellie looked up. "Megan! I didn't know you were in town! I haven't seen you for ages."

Megan smiled widely. "Annie needed some help for the Christmas rush, so here I am. But I didn't expect to see so many people from long ago. Tage is back for the holiday, too."

Megan had been a regular summer visitor, and had even come for a year of high school. Ellie vaguely remembered Tage, but the two were a couple years older than her. "Do you remember Wes Colton?" she asked, pointing down to where the cowboy was perusing pastries at the other end of the case.

"We've already met," Megan said. "He gave us a great sleigh ride the other day. And he's got an awfully cute...dog." She grinned wickedly.

Ellie laughed. "That he does."

"So do you know what you want? Besides him?"

"Megan!" Ellie blushed and looked down the room, surprised that Wes hadn't heard.

"I recognize the look in your eye. But besides that, what can I get you?"

Ellie inhaled deeply and willed the heat to leave her face. "I'd love a piece of the chocolate and pear *torta*, please."

At the end of the counter, Wes straightened. "And I'd like one of these puffy ball things here. With chocolate inside." He joined her back near the register, and Ellie watched him struggle to hide a smile.

Great. He had heard.

She kept her face down while Megan got their pastries and rang them up. Outside, Wes didn't say anything. Just kept his hand on her back and grinned widely as he ate his cream puff.

Ellie finally swallowed the last morsel of scrumptious *torta*. She sighed and looked at Wes. "You're extra cute with a chocolate cream mustache, Cowboy."

Wes swiped above his lip and licked his finger. "As cute as my...dog?"

Ellie groaned and playfully slapped his arm. "Beast."

"No, that's my cattle." He grinned.

She rolled her eyes and tucked her arm into his as they walked on.

Wes pointed out the latest *Adventfester* window on his sleigh ride route. Light shone through colored paper to show a manger scene, complete with sheep and camels around Baby Jesus and his parents.

"Sometimes I wish our sleigh rides went at night so people could see them," he said, "but I at least point them out and encourage them to drive past after dark."

"I think the Advent windows are the coolest part of the town's celebrations," Ellie said. "Something new to look forward to each night, but if you miss one, you can always see it the next night."

Wes smiled down at her. "You like it even more than the Santa Chase, or the tree lighting?"

"Oh yes. Those usher in the Christmas season, and they're exciting, but the Advent windows bring a joy that continues quietly. I think I like that the most."

Wes didn't answer, but reached out a leather-gloved hand to take her mittened one. His grip was strong and gentle at the same time, and warmed her throughout.

The flutter of excitement that he'd always brought on when they were young was still there. Ellie pondered the wonder of that—that after so many years, the feelings were still so strong. As if their love had only been put away for a season, like Christmas ornaments, and now were being brought out again.

And yet they weren't the same people. Parenthood had changed her in more ways than she could count, and she still carried some emotional wounds from her marriage. Not to mention the old scars from Wes leaving just as she had been envisioning a life together.

Had Wes felt the same emptiness when he'd left? Maybe. Who knew what guys felt and what they didn't? But he must have been feeling empty anyway, to go searching for something in life that he couldn't name.

And here he was back again. Still the same person she'd shared so many experiences with, still making her heart pound. Only now he seemed stronger, more purposeful.

More responsible? Less likely to hurt her again?

Only time would tell, but for now, her heart said she should give him that time.

"Penny for your thoughts," Wes asked.

"Mmm." Ellie wasn't going to blast those thoughts out in the open, but didn't quite know how much to share. "Just thinking about how we've changed," she finally said.

Wes was silent as they walked back toward the town center, and it was her turn to wonder where his mind was going. Finally he spoke. "We have, and we haven't."

Exactly what she'd been thinking. She looked up at him, but waited.

"It's kind of like training a horse," he continued. "They learn new things, they settle, they learn to trust you, but their personalities don't change. The friendly ones are still friendly, the silly ones are still silly, the ones who kick might not kick as much, but you still have to watch them."

He squeezed her hand. "You've been through some rough

times, and you have a lot of responsibilities now, but you're still fun and caring and generous. You should be proud."

Ellie walked quietly beside him for a moment. "Olivia has a lot to do with that."

They paused as they turned back toward the town center. Ellie looked over at another Advent window, this one with a family of snow people. "What about you? You've changed, I can tell, but…"

Wes gave a wry half-smile. "Not much, it seems. I still don't know what to do with my life. But I guess tending cattle has made me stick to things better. And accept things I can't change, like losing a certain number of calves during calving season, no matter how hard we try. I've had lots of time to think, too, but that hasn't gotten me anywhere."

Ellie led him on. "You obviously still love animals. And you love your Grandma, even if she's not here anymore."

Wes pulled her back to a stop, tugging one hand so she was facing him. His eyes were dark and intense, and the warm tingles from holding his hand again turned to a massive fluttering of baby chicks in Ellie's stomach. She hadn't seen that look in his eyes in a very long time.

Correction. She hadn't seen that look in his eyes *ever*. Calm, knowing, and deeply serious.

He reached up and pulled her knit cap down farther over her ear, his thumb brushing her jaw on the way. His face was so close she could feel his breath warm her cheeks.

"I do love animals, Ellie. And you're right, I still love my grandma." He nudged a piece of hair back under her cap. "But mostly, I love you. I never stopped."

He gazed at her, not moving closer. Ellie quivered, wanting him to kiss her, wanting to turn back the clock ten years. "I—I…" she stammered. There were no words for the sensations running through her body and the tumult of thoughts tumbling about in her mind. She wanted to both leap into his arms and fly far away from him at the same time.

Wes brushed the back of his glove against her cheek. "You don't need to say anything, sweetheart. You just need to hear. And feel."

Oh, did she feel! Confusion. Excitement. Anticipation. And more confusion.

He loved her still. And yet…would it make a difference to his plans? Would he still go back to the Black Rock ranch? Like a teenager, would he leave her again?

And why couldn't she just spit the words out and ask?

She looked in his eyes, saw the grown-up love shining out for all the world to see. For her to see. And believe.

He leaned forward and kissed her other cheek, his lips soft and warm against her cold skin.

How good it felt. How right. She wouldn't risk her heart for any other man, but all those feelings that had lain dormant for nine years were as strong as ever once she let them out. It wasn't like with Marshall, whom she had hardly known when she married him. She wouldn't need years to realize she was in love with him, and that he was worth hanging onto.

He was her Wes. He was the man he hadn't been before, and he still loved her.

Wes nodded toward the town square with its sparkling trees and brightly-lit carousel.

He wanted to walk on, and she wanted to stay standing close to him. She shook her head slightly, and he raised an eyebrow.

She gazed up at him, knowing what she wanted was written on her face.

This tall cowboy of hers obliged and lowered his lips to hers, softly, gently.

JEN PETERS

Ellie kissed him back in wonder, inhaling his familiar scent, feeling suddenly, wonderfully at home.

Wes pulled back and smiled, his eyes gleaming. "Well now, ma'am," he said in a put-on cowboy drawl, "you sure do know how to warm a man up."

He brushed one more feather-light kiss across her lips, then tucked her hand in his arm and walked on across the square. At the base of her apartment stairs, he kissed her lightly again, touched his fingers to the brim of his hat, and said, "Tomorrow?"

Ellie nodded silently, her mitten pressed to her tingling lips. He turned to go, but she grabbed his arm and pulled him back, pulled his head down to hers.

This wasn't the gentle kiss of earlier. This was demanding, possessive, sending her soaring through the limitless sky, bringing her back down to earth, then sending her soaring again. The world dropped away while she reveled in the feel of his lips, the touch of his hands in her hair, the peppermint and Wes taste of him.

He was heaven. He was home. He was hers.

Wes pulled away first, and she opened her eyes to see his face filled with love and desire. "I'd better go," he whispered roughly.

He bent to pick up her knit cap from where it had landed. He took long moments to put it on her and tuck her hair in, his gaze never leaving hers.

Ellie's breath hitched. She tipped forward for another kiss, but Wes just smiled and took a step back. She watched him go, then floated up the stairs to where Abby had already put Olivia to bed.

Yes, hers.

10

Wes paced back and forth across the living room, hands in pockets, mumbling under his breath. Kuda watched from the entryway, his head resting on his stretched out legs, but his eyes moving with every circuit Wes made.

Last night had been magical…the walk, the snow, Ellie's hand in his. And the sense that she was finally seeing him as he was now, not as he had been back in high school.

And those kisses! He'd kissed a few women over the years, sometimes probably hotter and heavier than he should have, but Ellie's first feather touches had made his heart pound like it never had before. And then she had pulled him back…

Wes had never felt as wanted or as needed as he had then. Ellie had looked at him with hope glowing from those perfect green eyes. Like they could have a future together. Like maybe he wasn't chasing a pipe dream after all. Like there might be a permanent Wes and Ellie.

Wes and Ellie Colton.

His lungs suddenly couldn't get enough air. His legs refused to move another step.

The thought of the two of them together, married… sitting on a porch swing, Olivia between them…waking up next to Ellie, her belly huge with his own baby…teaching a son or daughter to ride a pony…growing old together, still loving each other's gnarled hands and lined faces.

Wes sank onto the couch. The vision was so real, so complete that he couldn't imagine anything else. He'd always known he wanted a family someday, but hadn't realized his dream could only be fulfilled with Ellie. No other woman in the world could ever take her place.

He wished once again that he had known that nine years ago, that he had never left Huckleberry Falls, but at least he knew it now.

Wes stood again, slapped his cowboy hat against his thigh and called Kuda. "Come on, boy. We can enjoy the dreams while we sleep."

HE UNLOADED Sadie from the trailer the next day, his murmurs to her filled with joy. He harnessed her to the sleigh, his hands working smoothly, the bubbles inside him carrying over to the mare, who perked her ears every time he spoke.

Wes couldn't help it. His mind and heart swirled with thoughts of Ellie, her touch, her kiss. The wonder of it all.

She could be his.

Please, God, please let her be his.

"Wes Colton! I'm here for a sleigh ride!"

He whipped around to see Abby McKean. Ellie's big sister.

Ellie's *protective* big sister, now looking like a mama bear whose cubs were threatened.

"Hi, Abby. Long time, no see." He kept his voice even and pleasant.

"Can you have me back before my lunch hour ends?" Abby's voice was even, too, but he could sense the grizzly underneath it.

"Hop in. The regular route takes about twenty minutes, but I can shorten it if you want."

"Twenty minutes is fine," Abby said as she clambered into the sleigh.

Wes handed her the rug to put over her legs, but she didn't say anything else. He shrugged and pulled himself into the driver's seat, picking up the reins as he went.

He slapped them lightly against Sadie's rump. "Walk on." Sadie leaned into the harness, and they glided easily forward. "I don't suppose I need to point out the carousel or tell you what *Adventfester* is."

He glanced back, but Abby just sat with her arms crossed.

Okay, then. It was obvious she had something to say, but he'd just let her be until she was ready. His mind came up with various scenarios, but he focused on Sadie instead of borrowing trouble.

For an eighteen-year-old horse, Sadie was still strong and well muscled. They had bonded over grooming and treats, and he wouldn't mind taking her home with him.

Home. Where was home now? Back at Black Rock? Here in Huckleberry Falls? With what as his future?

"What are you doing here, Wes?" Abby's voice came from the back, as self-righteous as he remembered.

Huh. He hadn't expected to be thinking the same thing she was. "I'm closing up my grandmother's house. I'm sure Ellie told you."

"You know what I mean. You and Ellie."

"Seems to me that's between her and me." Logical big sister or not, this was not her business.

Abby huffed. "Look, could you pull over and look at me? I can't talk to the back of your cowboy hat."

Wes grimaced, but he may as well get this over with. He pulled Sadie to a stop in front of a yellow Victorian house dripping with Christmas wreaths.

He turned in the seat. "Say what you're going to say, Abby. You won't rest until you do."

She huffed again, brushing her carrot-colored hair out of her face. "You and Ellie were the greatest thing on earth in high school, and we were all worried about you guys being too serious, too young," Abby finally spit out. "And then you went and broke her heart."

"You're right."

"You have to—wait, what?"

Wes looked Abby full in the face. "You're right. I left, and I broke her heart. And I was young and dumb enough not to realize it."

"Oh." Abby deflated for a moment, then gathered her indignation again. "So what are you doing here? You're only going to break her heart again."

Wes shook his head. "I won't. I will never make that mistake again."

"She's falling in love with you again. Don't deny it—I can see it all over her face."

Wes kept his face still, kept the hope bursting out of him hidden from her.

"So?" Abby pushed.

He shrugged. "I love her," he said simply. "I always have, I just pushed it away for a while."

Abby's face was hard as she studied him. "Her home is here."

"I know."

"Are you staying?"

94

"Of course. I—" Wes broke off. If he were honest, he really didn't know what he was going to do.

Abby stood in the sleigh. Wes felt Sadie pick up a foot and put it down again.

"You *don't* know, do you?" Abby demanded. "And you've got no right to get Ellie's hopes up until you figure out what's most important to you and what you're going to do about it."

"I just...Ellie and I need to talk," Wes stammered.

"Ellie and you need to cool it for a while. Now, before she's as much in love with you as ever. She won't recover from another broken heart."

Wes was silent for long moments. Sadie shifted her weight, then settled again. "I love her," he finally said.

Abby's voice softened. "I know you do, Wes. But she's my little sister, and I won't stand by and see her hurt again. You need to figure things out before this goes any further."

She thumped back in her seat and pulled the rug over her again.

Wes turned forward. He felt gut-punched. He did love Ellie. He wanted the rest of his life to be with her. But Abby was right—he needed to figure things out.

He slowly gathered Sadie's reins and jiggled them. "Walk on."

TENSE AND CHILLED, Ellie stood outside La Chevelure's back door at noon on Wednesday, her day off that week. Wes and the sleigh were gone—he must have customers already—and she had to admit she'd been longing to see him again. Even though that incredible kiss had only been last night. Her soul swelled inside with the surety of the feeling. The rightness of being together with Wes had hit her like a loaded semi, pushing her along and rolling over any apprehensions she might have.

She shut the feelings down, tucking them away to pull out later, and took a deep breath. Alice had asked to meet with her, and for all her preparation, a herd of buffalo stampeded through her stomach. Second thoughts tumbled around her mind: could she really afford this? Was she ready to settle into a permanent business? Was she too inexperienced to be a business owner?

But it was her dream that was falling into her lap here, and the exhilaration outweighed the nerves.

Alice arrived and actually let a half-smile appear on her face. Ellie followed her into the office and perched on the edge of the visitor's chair.

Alice settled behind her desk and pulled a folder of papers to the center. "Shall we begin?"

Ellie nodded, pulling her own folder out of her bag.

"There are some other things to factor in," Alice said, "but this is what my accountant could put together fairly quickly." She passed a set of papers across to Ellie.

Ellie looked at them carefully, noting the gross sales, the salaries and commissions, and the cost of all their products. Another page showed the lease amount, utilities, insurance, and a few other things, and another broke the payroll expenses down even further. At the end were a few pages of graphs that would take some time to study.

"This seems very complete," Ellie said. She straightened the papers, then gathered her courage for the next question. "If I can ask a more personal question, why are you leaving? And when?"

Alice almost smiled. "January 20th. Even if we come to an agreement quickly, I may need to sign the final papers by mail. I don't know if they'd be ready by the time I leave."

"Um, can I ask? You have a great business here. Why are you leaving Huckleberry Falls?"

The familiar hard set of Alice's mouth reappeared. "Private reasons. Nothing to do with the business."

Ellie nodded. It would take an act of God for Alice to admit something about her personal life. She was an odd woman to be a hair stylist, but it took all kinds, right?

Alice stood. "Get some advice on those," she said, gesturing toward the papers. "I'll have the final figures for you on Friday. Shall we meet before the salon opens?"

"Sure. Eight o'clock?"

Alice agreed, and Ellie danced her way out the back door. It was only a mental dance—she wouldn't want to make a fool of herself in front of her boss—but the excitement overwhelmed her by the time she reached the car.

She scuffed her snow boots around, did a bit of a jig and gave a fist pump, then straightened her coat and waited until she was in the car before she shouted, "YES!"

On Main Street, Ellie slowed to match the speed of Wes's sleigh. "Hey there, cowboy!" she called through her open window.

Wes turned to her and grinned, but didn't say anything.

"I'll be at Mom's tonight, but see you tomorrow?"

Wes tipped his hat to her. Ellie grinned as she watched the two young women in back fan themselves. *He's all mine, girls, all mine.*

She blew him a kiss and drove on. Her satisfied and rather smug feelings had her singing Christmas carols at the top of her lungs.

THE BARN WAS quiet as Wes led Sadie in. He was too used to the horses all being in for the night by the time he got back from the sleigh rides. He enjoyed the tasks, though. Made him feel at home.

He gave Sadie a good rubdown, putting his muscles into not only grooming her, but relaxing muscles and scratching her favorite spots. Once she was back in her stall, he mixed and distributed grain for nineteen horses and put a flake of alfalfa in each manger. Thank goodness Steve had automatic waterers in the stalls.

Finally ready, he led Scamp and Blackie in from outside. Scamp nosed his pocket, but he had neither sugar cubes or carrots with him. Wes smiled as the gelding dove for his grain instead—it didn't take much to make him happy.

Wes opened five stall doors down the other side—the long-timers knew exactly which stall was theirs and would head straight for it. Outside, he hunched against the wind as he swung the wide gate to let them through. All five pranced in, excited by the breeze and the prospect of dinner.

He brought the other horses in by twos and threes, and Olivia's pony came last. With a gash along her side.

Dang.

Daisy settled into her hay, nonchalant about it all, while Wes ran his hands over her body. He found a minor cut on her fetlock, but no extra injuries to speak of. Just a long line across her ribs that oozed blood slowly. The last six inches widened into a cut that bled freely and would need stitches. She must have found something in the pasture to scrape against.

He called Dr. Janssen while he went to the tack room for some clean cloths. With pressure on the wound and waiting for the vet to arrive, he steeled himself to call Ellie. Was she as tender-hearted as she used to be?

He needn't have worried. Ellie's number went straight to voicemail, and he remembered she was with her mother. Wes left a message asking her to come to the barn without Olivia, hung up, then called back to tell her it was a minor injury, not life-threatening. He didn't want her panicking.

Phone calls over, he adjusted the cloth against Daisy's wound and ran his other hand down her neck. "You'll be just fine, little girl," he murmured.

Daisy kept her head down, ignoring him in favor of her hay.

He smiled at the pony's resilience. Most of the horses he knew would at least be fidgeting, not because they were in intense pain, but because he was pressing on a sore place. He wondered if he'd be as unconcerned about something that hurt.

Dr. Janssen bustled into the barn half an hour later. "Wes, good. I can only stay to stitch her up, but you can do the clean-up after. I've got a mare colicking across town, and her heart rate is still high even with the analgesics and oil. We may need to take her in."

"Surgery?"

"I hope not, but maybe."

Wes shook his head. "I guess I've been lucky. Haven't had any colic that wouldn't respond to walking and Banamine."

Dr. Janssen gave him a wry look as he pulled a suture kit from his bag. "You probably keep a closer eye on your animals, too. This one was down and rolling enough she's got a kink in her gut that probably won't straighten on its own, plus the impaction."

Wes moved to Daisy's head as Dr. Janssen examined her. "See here," the vet pointed. "Whatever it was tore deeply first, then lightened as she moved away from it. But we need to dig around and make sure there's no debris left."

Wes stroked Daisy's nose and murmured soothing nothings to her as Dr. Janssen probed the cut, giving a *hmmm* and an *uh huh* once in a while, then, "Ah hah!" He pulled a splinter out, and then a tiny piece of bark. "I'd guess she met up with a broken branch."

"I'll check the pasture when we're done." Wes looked outside at the darkness. "Or tomorrow, when I can see. I'll make sure the morning guy doesn't turn them out until I do."

Dr. Janssen cleaned the pony's wound, then stitched it neatly. He handed Wes a bottle of penicillin. "You have needles and syringes?"

"I think so. If not, I can get some."

The vet rummaged in his bag and pulled two out, grimacing as he checked his watch. "Give her 5 cc's now, daily for four days. I have to go. Call me if it starts an infection anyway. Keep it open to the air and dry."

"Okay to turn her out in the morning?"

"If it's dry weather and she's anxious, yes. Otherwise just in the arena a few times a day. She needs to move lightly, but we don't want her getting colic, too."

Dr. Janssen hurried back to his truck. Daisy shifted her weight a few times, then settled back into her hay. Wes got an alcohol swab from the vet kit in the tack room, gave the pony her shot, and settled in to wait for Ellie.

An hour, two voice messages and two *Call me* texts later, he finally motioned Kuda to the truck and drove home.

11

The wind had blown most of the snow off the roads by the time Ellie headed to her mom's that evening. She'd made batch upon batch of cookies until it was time to pick Olivia up from school. This whole salon business was just too exciting to stay still.

"I brought Applejack for Sarah to play with," Olivia said from the back, "and Twilight Sparkle for me."

Ellie smiled. "Sarah doesn't have enough ponies of her own?"

"She doesn't have Applejack! This will make her happy."

The whole family was getting together for dinner, and Ellie wanted a serious talk afterwards while the girls played. What would her mother and Abby think of the business proposal? Had they realized how serious she was when she'd mentioned it before? Would they try to talk her out of it like they tried to talk her out of Wes?

"Hey, Honey," her mom greeted her from the front door. "And my little Christmas elf!"

"Grandma!" Olivia ran for a hug. Ellie gathered her purse,

the folder of papers, and the salad for dinner, and followed them in.

Abby was already there, helping Sarah get out the My Little Pony castle that Grandma kept. "So what's this about, El?"

"What? We can't have dinner together?" Ellie grinned.

"You were way too serious for just dinner, O Daughter of Mine," Mrs. McKean said. "Talk now or after dinner?"

Abby laughed. "Look at Ellie—she'll burst if we wait until after dinner!"

Ellie felt herself blush. "C'mere. I have something to show you." She glanced at the girls, already engrossed with the ponies, and sat at the table. She pulled her papers out. "Remember I told you about wanting to buy the salon?"

"Yeah, dreaming again," Abby said.

"Let her talk," Mrs. McKean warned.

Ellie took a deep breath. "I think it's going to happen. Alice gave me these today." She spread the papers out with pride.

Her mother and sister examined them, trading pages as needed.

"This will be hundreds of thousands of dollars, Ellie!" her mother gasped.

Ellie nodded. "But I won't be doing it by myself."

Abby was silent. Finally she said, "It looks like it makes a good profit, but you did see the loan she's got, didn't you?"

"Loan?" Ellie gulped.

"Nearly ninety thousand still owing," Abby said, tapping her fingernail on a number.

Ellie blanched. She took the page from her sister, wondering if her dream had just gone down the drain.

"That's not all bad," Abby said. "I would think that would be subtracted from the normal purchase price. But still, you'd have those payments to make on top of your own. And payroll and supplies."

Ellie stared at the figures. "Mom?"

Mrs. McKean shook her head. "What I know about business wouldn't fill a teaspoon. I just know you need to have all the information before you make a decision."

"And you need to have your head on straight when you do," Abby added. "You'll be talking to Mrs. Jackson, right? Merry's mother?"

"Of course."

"Good. She knows what she's doing." Abby paused for a moment. "If you buy the salon, what about Wes?"

Ellie looked up sharply. "Wes is excited for me."

"I know," Abby said. "And I know he's falling in love with you again."

He was?

He was. Ellie suddenly knew it for truth.

"But…" Abby's voice was gentle. "What are you going to do if he goes back to Colorado?"

"He won't." Ellie put more confidence into her voice than she really felt. "He knows he doesn't want to be a rancher the rest of his life." Whatever he did, if he was really falling in love with her, wouldn't he want to stay close? And why, oh why hadn't she forced the question?

The children's voices sounded over the adults' silence. Then Sarah said, "No! Applejack can be there! She doesn't have to stay on the farm all the time."

Mrs. McKean pushed up from the chair. "I think it's time to get dinner on. Come on, kids, you can help me get the silverware."

Dinnertime conversation ranged from kindergarten and pre-school activities to the bird houses Mrs. McCarthy put on her outdoor Christmas tree this year, but Ellie stayed mostly silent.

She was falling in love again, too. And if Wes was, if it wasn't just a fling, what were his plans?

Ellie gasped at the end of the evening when she turned her phone back on. Two texts and two missed calls from Wes. She tapped his number. "Wes, it's me. How's Daisy?"

"Daisy?" said a sleepy Olivia beside her.

"She'll be fine." Wes's deep voice rumbled through her concern and into her heart.

"Mommy, what's wrong with Daisy?" Olivia was wide awake now.

"Mr. Wes says she'll be okay, sweetie." Ellie turned back to the phone. "What happened?"

"Came in tonight with a gash on her side. I had Dr. Janssen out to stitch it up."

"But she's okay? Can we go see her?"

She could almost see Wes shrug, but what must be an everyday happening for him was somewhat alarming for her. "Sure," he said. "I'll meet you there."

✶✶✶

WES ENTERED THE DIM BARN, leaving one of the big doors slightly open. He inhaled deeply, the smell of hay and horse as welcoming as always. He flicked the overhead lights on, and horses nickered and hung their heads over the stall doors. He gave pats and rubs on his way down to Daisy's stall.

Olivia came running in before he reached the pony.

"Daisy! Daisy!" she cried.

"Walk, young lady!" Ellie called after her. "You know you don't run in the barn."

Wes smiled as the girl shifted smoothly into a gait that

would put a race walker to shame. She reached him within seconds.

"Did Daisy get cut bad? Is she going to be okay?"

Wes took her hand and walked the rest of the way with her. "She'll be just fine. She's a tough little pony, you know."

Olivia gasped when Wes opened the stall door. She approached slowly, reaching a finger out to touch the bold, black stitches. "Oh, Daisy, it must hurt so bad," she crooned.

Daisy turned to sniff Olivia.

Ellie caught up to them. She stood in the doorway with Wes, her very presence warming him, and tucked her hand in his arm. "Does she get painkillers? Does she even need them?"

Wes shook his head. "Might be a little tender, but that's all. She'll be just fine."

"Like you said," Ellie responded. "I'm sorry if we overreacted."

She could overreact anytime she wanted, if it put her cuddling up next to him. He liked the idea of protecting her, of having strength that she could lean on.

Olivia petted Daisy's soft nose for a minute, then Ellie said, "Come on, sweetie, we need to go. It's way past your bedtime."

"Mom, can't I sleep here with Daisy? She'll be lonely if she's by herself."

"Olivia," Ellie warned.

Wes smiled at her "mom" voice. His own mother had had to use that tone on him quite a few times.

"But Mom, she's hurting so much! I don't like being by myself when I'm sick. Daisy won't like it either." Olivia began to pout.

"I'll tell you what," Wes said before everyone became unhappy. "How about if I show you some roping tricks for a minute, and you can see that Daisy's okay by herself?"

Olivia jumped and clapped her hands, startling the pony. She shoved her hand over her mouth, then lifted it to stroke Daisy's neck and apologize.

Ellie gave Wes a warning look. "We can't take very long. It's quite late for her."

"Not long," Wes promised. He gave Daisy half a flake of grass hay, then retrieved his lariat from behind the seat of his truck. "Can you bring that empty bucket, Olivia?" he asked, pointing. "Now put it upside down in the arena."

He chuckled to himself—this was likely to be embarrassing and hilarious. He kept most of his rope in his left hand and a large loop in his right. He swung it smoothly over his head, his wrist twisting nicely, and heard Uncle Dirt's voice in his head as he released it.

To land right next to the overturned bucket. Not even touching it.

Ellie smiled encouragingly. Olivia giggled.

Once more: the rope circling overhead, release, and…miss.

Four more unsuccessful tries, until both Ellie and Olivia were laughing. Hilarious was the right word. Or else pathetic.

"I told you I was the world's worst at roping." This time he didn't mind, though. He was putting smiles on his girls' faces.

Ellie grinned. "Maybe you need a different target?"

"Oh yeah?" He raised an eyebrow and turned to Olivia. "Maybe a six-year-old target?"

"Yes! Yes! Rope *me*!" Olivia stepped far away from her mother. "Just in case he misses."

Ellie folded her arms and pursed her lips, but didn't say no.

Wes swung the lariat again, smiling at Olivia's scrunched up face. He released.

"You lassoed me!" the young girl cried.

Wes's jaw went slack. He had actually roped her.

"I don't believe it," Ellie said.

He grinned. "Neither do I. I mean, sometimes I can rope a bucket, but not often. It's the wind, or the stiffness of my rope, or—"

"Something with your eye-hand coordination?" Ellie put in. "Like you should have played baseball instead of the trumpet?"

"What now?" Olivia asked.

"We-ll," Wes drawled, looking at the loop of rope laying in the dirt, "if you were a calf, I'd snug that rope right up and pull you to me. But since the vet doesn't need to check you over, and I'm not planning to brand you, I'll just collect it and say that's a good way to end for the night."

Olivia started to pout again. "But Daisy—"

Wes shook his head. "We'll check on her. You'll be surprised."

Sure enough, Daisy didn't lift her head from her hay, no matter how much Olivia tried to get her attention. "You're right, Mr. Wes, she's not lonely!"

Ellie snuggled into his side again, and Wes thought he could die happy right now. A beautiful, loving woman in his arms, a girl who hero-worshipped him, and a heart so full it was brimming over.

Now he just had to figure out how to make it all work.

12

In the shadow of the basement corner, hidden behind what Wes had thought was the last of his grandmother's boxes, he spied a familiar outline. The metal-reinforced corners, a glimpse of a latch…it was his old trumpet.

He pulled the case over the box of papers and jogged upstairs with it. Anticipation overtook him—would it still play? He opened the case and his breath escaped in a whoosh. The previously shiny brass was now tarnished, but the velvet lining had protected it from dust and debris. He picked it up, rubbed the mouthpiece with his t-shirt and inserted it. Ran the valve keys to warm up his fingers. Raised the trumpet to his mouth, took a deep breath, and blew.

The sound of a sick cow burst forth.

Kuda howled a song in response.

Wes settled on the couch, laughing at the reminder of his first attempts at music in the sixth grade. "You going to provide harmony for me, Kuda?"

The Husky sat at his feet, attentive and ready.

Wes played again, this time getting some recognizable

notes while Kuda sang along. He ran a couple of scales, his fingers and mouth slow and rusty, then played pieces of some songs he remembered.

Other memories came back. Going up to the lookout above Huckleberry Falls with Ellie, kissing some, but mostly just hanging out. Sometimes Ellie would have a book to read while he practiced band parts, or she'd run her fingers through his hair while he played, distracting him until he stopped and paid attention to her. She had tried the trumpet a time or two, but came up with the same sick cow sound he just had. They had laughed each time, ending up snuggling with soft kisses.

Wes set the trumpet back in its case, his lips and cheeks sore from the unaccustomed work. The memories and wobbly music had been fun, but he'd be better off keeping his mouth for kissing these days.

Thoughts of Ellie energized him, and he trotted back down to the basement for that last box. He blew the dust off it, coughed, and opened it up to find bills, receipts and souvenirs from the seventies and eighties. He shook his head in disbelief. "Why does anybody need to keep electric bills longer than I've been alive?"

Kuda looked up, voiced a soft song, and settled his head back on his front legs.

"Yeah, that's what I think, boy." Wed pulled an empty box to him and started dumping papers by the handful. He paused at some small items: 1977 movie ticket stubs to Star Wars, a brochure from Fisherman's Wharf in San Francisco, and a blank postcard of Pike's Peak.

"You did get out and have some fun, didn't you Grandma?" He looked over to the picture of her and Grandpa when they were young. That would be one thing he'd keep.

Unless he found more boxes, Wes was finally done with

the papers. It felt more bittersweet than he'd expected. One person's life literally summed up by bags and boxes of things to burn. The thought made his heart heavier than he'd expected.

The pictures, though—they showed Grandma's real life. They would keep memories alive. And then there was his dad and himself. They were proof that Grandma had lived well, weren't they?

Wes wasn't sure. After Mom died, his dad's life had kind of gone down the tubes. He'd married Bimbo Barbie, ignored his son, and then when he'd finally called it quits on that marriage, Dad had taken the overseas job. Still distancing himself from everyone.

And Wes himself? What had he achieved with his life? Nine years drifting from ranch to ranch, leaving the girl he loved behind, and having nothing to show for it but an affinity for horses.

Ellie had suggested he think about becoming a veterinarian. Treating injured animals—more than the basic bandages and penicillin shots he did already. Stitching cuts, healing overworked tendons, helping mares with difficult births, preventing founder. Actually, he did some of that now, but to have proper training and skills, to be in charge of an animal's care instead of just helping…

"What do you think, Kuda? Would I make a good vet?"

The Husky came and nuzzled under his arm, then settled with his head on Wes's leg.

"This isn't going to be very comfortable, you know." Wes eased over, still sitting on the floor but now leaning against the couch. His thoughts kept going.

If he were a vet, would he specialize in horses, or large animals in general, or dogs and cats, too? He wouldn't mind dogs. Cats would be iffy, though, and he shuddered at the thought of treating a hamster or gerbil. Rodents were rodents, after all, no matter if kids thought they were cute.

Wes daydreamed for a while, envisioning himself in Dr. Sue's place back at the ranch, coming out in the hot summer sun for a colt that had cut his leg, in the middle of the night for a foaling mare in distress, or working to keep pink eye from spreading through the herd.

He liked it. He really could see himself being a vet instead of a ranch hand the rest of his life. Enjoying a real career, and actually being able to support a family. Would that make Ellie happy, too?

He patted Kuda and moved to get up, feeling tingles in a few choice spots. "Numb bum," he told the dog. Kuda howled a short song back to him.

Wes worked his way to his feet, made a few trips up and down the hall to get his circulation going again, then pulled out his phone to look up vet school information.

An hour later, discouragement had replaced his anticipation. It would take four years and top grades to even get into vet school. And then it was four more years of study —microbiology, anatomy for multiple species, pharmacology, and more, all sounding intimidating.

Could he do it? He hadn't been terrible in high school, but he wasn't a brainiac either. And he'd been away from it for nearly a decade. How much would it take to even get ready for Chem 101?

Wes dropped his head in his hands. "It seems impossible, Grandma," he said into the empty air. "I wish you were here to talk to."

One of Grandma's favorite phrases came into his mind. *How do you eat an elephant?*

"I know, I know," he muttered. "One bite at a time. One problem at a time." He looked at Kuda, laying on the floor with ears perked at the sound of Wes's voice. But he wasn't a teenager anymore—he was quite capable of analyzing the facts and making a plan. "Okay, Kuda, first problem: college might be too hard."

It's not a weakness to ask for help. Another Grandma-ism.

She was usually right, though. There must be tutors available. And probably some online help programs.

"Workable, Kuda. Probably not easy, but not impossible. As long as my tutor isn't like Mrs. Cornelius from fourth grade."

The Husky stretched and padded over to sit by his feet.

"Going to help me, huh?" Wes scratched behind his ears, and Kuda promptly rolled over for a belly rub.

Wes obliged, rubbing and talking. "So you're part of the next problem. I don't think I can do these classes and hold a job at the same time. Think you can earn some money?"

Kuda rolled back over and plopped his head down.

"Yeah, I didn't think so. So let's get back to work on the house while I think."

Wes checked the loose boards on the back deck and measured for the railing pieces that needed replacing. By the time he had finished cutting lumber, he'd worked out that he could probably take less than the normal load of classes each semester, at least until vet school. It would stretch his undergrad out, but he should be able to hold close to a full-time job while he did it.

What he didn't know was how he would pay for it all. Financial aid would help, but he couldn't count on a lot of it. And vet school itself—expensive!

And where would he be? Huckleberry Falls didn't have a university, let alone a vet school. There was only one place for a veterinary degree in Wyoming, and it was clear over in Laramie, the opposite corner of the state.

And then there was Ellie. If he wanted anything long-term with her...heck with "long-term." He may as well admit to the feeling that had been growing: he wanted something permanent. He'd loved her before, and that love had only been hidden away. It was back full force, and he didn't want to blow any possibility of showing her he'd changed, showing her he was worth a second chance.

But college and vet school would take him away, abandoning her once again.

Or could she be interested in a long-distance relationship?

Wes tried to picture himself in an apartment somewhere trying to study and work, his only contact with her being on the phone. He tried to picture her here in Huckleberry Falls, running the salon and still single-parenting.

He thought of the people he knew and the stories he'd heard about cross-country relationships. Trying to find time to connect around different schedules—his dad was a good example of how that didn't work well. Trying to keep the romance in place when you're miles apart. Reading on-screen facial clues to try to tell what the other was really feeling.

He buried his face in Kuda's fur. His love for Ellie was precious; hopefully she felt the same way.

Was there a way they could make it work?

13

Olivia danced with excitement outside the Christmas Market. "It's snowing again!" she cried, holding her mittens out to catch the flakes falling from the evening sky. "And Mr. Wes is coming shopping with us and I get to pick out a present for Grandma and it's the most *scrumptious* day ever!"

"Scrumptious?" Ellie echoed. "Who taught you a day could be scrumptious?"

"Aunt Abby. She said a day could be whatever feeling we want. And *scrumptious* is my new word."

Abby said that? Her sister, the practical pessimist? No, not a pessimist exactly, just someone whose life wasn't at all what she had planned.

For that matter, Ellie's life wasn't what she had planned, either. Although she was closer to it now than she had been in New York. She had Olivia, she was buying the salon, and Wes...maybe she had Wes.

He was making progress on the house, although she knew it was slower than he had planned. It was because he was such a generous guy—taking over the sleigh rides and now doing the evening chores for Uncle Steve. She loved him for that.

She let the thought reverberate through her body, and felt it settle. She loved him. He was kind, giving, gentle and fun with Olivia, and oh-so-handsome. But would he stay? Could he see more possibilities than being a ranch hand the rest of his life?

"Mommy! There's Mr. Wes!" Olivia pointed.

Sure enough, a black Stetson bobbed above the crowd. Wes was suddenly there, a soft smile on his face, his heavy rancher's coat keeping him warm. "How did I ever agree to go Christmas shopping with you on a crowded night?"

Ellie linked her arm in his. "Because you couldn't stay away?"

"You're right there, darlin'." He said it with a cowboy twang, and Ellie smiled.

"You're a real, live cowboy, aren't you Mr. Wes? Even if you're not a good lasso-er?" Olivia tugged on his jacket.

He crouched beside her. "I sure am, Miss Olivia, and I roped you, didn't I? And I think you're a real, live, Christmas-shopping girl, aren't you?"

"Yup!" She twirled around, her white coat spinning out, then jumped in his arms for a hug. "I love you, Mr. Wes."

The smile dropped off Ellie's face. Did she want her daughter feeling that way toward Wes so soon?

She held her breath while she waited for his response.

"You're mighty special too, pumpkin," he said. He let go of Olivia, stood, and inhaled deeply. "Let's do this."

They went into the Christmas Market, a row of joined buildings that held produce and baked goods in the summer, but were now filled with Christmas goodies. The air was rich with the scent of fudge and fir, and carols played lightly over the sound system.

Olivia stopped to eye the candy apples. "Please, Mommy? It would taste really good."

"I'm sure. *Scrumptious*, even." Ellie smiled. "But don't you think you should see all the different treats before you decide?"

"I guess," Olivia said mournfully.

They walked on, and Wes took Ellie's hand. "Anything in particular you're looking for?"

His hand felt so good in hers. So *right*. Her emotions were a roller coaster of confusion today. "Something unique for Mom and Abby," she answered, "although I've got their main presents. What about you?"

Wes shrugged. "Dad's still in Bahrain and it's too late to send anything. Maybe something for the Black family. I could take it back to the ranch with me."

There it was again. Ellie looked at him. His voice seemed quiet, dampened somehow, but his face didn't show anything moody. Was he feeling the uncertainty, too?

They browsed through carved nativity sets, hand-painted elves, small lap quilts and huge bed quilts, and woodcuts of cute sayings. The candy section ranged from fudge to popcorn to hand-dipped chocolate, and they had to drag Olivia away. "On the way out," Ellie reminded her.

Old-fashioned train sets filled one corner, and they stopped to watch the engine pick up coal cars and take them around the loop. "I had one of those when I was a kid," Wes said.

"Do you still have it?" Olivia asked. "Can we get it out?"

"Oh, no. I didn't have a place to keep it when Dad sold the house, so all my old stuff went to Goodwill."

How sad. Ellie knew her mother still had boxes of her childhood treasures in the attic, and Olivia could read the same books she had—Nancy Drew, Goosebumps, the Black

Stallion, all her favorites. Her collection of Breyer horses was up there, too, and it was probably time to pull them down.

They continued on, but didn't stop long at the jewelry displays or the carved-leather belts. Olivia had a tough decision to make as they worked their way back: chunky fudge or the original candy apple? She was chattering about the qualities of each when a wall saying caught Ellie's eye.

Be a flamingo in a flock of pigeons, in hot pink—perfect for conformist Abby.

"I need this!" Ellie said. She paid for it, plus a smoothly flowing, one-piece carving of Joseph, Mary and Jesus for her mother.

She caught up to Olivia and Wes at the quilts. Wes was admiring a blue and green log cabin design. "You like that?"

He shrugged and turned away. "I thought I might send it to the Blacks, but it's expensive, and I really need to watch my money. Did you find what you wanted?"

Ellie nodded, puzzled over his downcast mood. She had rarely seen him so quiet. She took his hand. "Want to talk about it?"

He gave a half-smile. "Nothing to talk about. Olivia, did you decide on the candy apple?"

"Yup! It's going to be sticky and crunchy and *scrumptious!*"

Ellie bought one for each of them, and they bit into the sticky-crunchy-scrumptiousness outside.

Wes looked up at the snow falling. "I guess I'd better go. Got work to do." He gave her a peck on the lips and walked away.

Ellie looked after him, not knowing what to think.

Olivia's humming changed to singing through sticky teeth. "All I want for Christmas is Mr. Wes for my daddy, Mr. Wes for my daddy…"

Ellie stilled, frozen by her daughter's words. A protective instinct rose through her, her Mama Bear personality coming out more fiercely than it had since they'd returned to Huckleberry Falls.

She hadn't dated at all since the divorce. Wes was the first man in Olivia's life other than her father, who had never paid much attention to her. Of course she was going to bond with Wes. He was kind, fun, and a cowboy, to boot.

And when Wes finished his grandmother's house and left for Colorado again?

It wasn't only Ellie's heart at risk, it was her daughter's.

14

Saturday was quickly becoming a day kissed by blessings. Ellie had re-done her business proposal after going through all the details and possibilities with Merry and her mother. She'd been at the bank doors when they opened this morning, and while the loan officer was hesitant to loan money to Ellie since she had no track record, he was happy to see Merry's substantial contribution. As long as the partnership paperwork was done, and Merry's portion could be collateral for the loan, the bank would have no problem financing the purchase.

Ellie gave a fist-pump as she exited. Only five clients that day, and then Wes wanted to do something. She wasn't sure what, but her mother was picking Olivia up from daycare, so she had the whole evening to have fun. And fun it would be —no doubts allowed.

She was going to buy La Chevelure. The words repeated in her mind throughout the day, while she was putting foils on a client's hair, giving someone a trim, cleaning up her station. Mrs. McCarthy came in, wanting her gray hair highlighted for Christmas, but Ellie didn't dare say anything. Not until she and Alice had settled on a price and signed papers, and maybe not even then.

As it was, she had to keep the anticipation off her face—her regular clients would be able to see her excitement, and she wouldn't be able to keep from blurting it out. But…*La Chevelure was going to be hers!*

"Wes seems awfully lonely at the house," Mrs. McCarthy said, looking pointedly at Ellie.

"He's working hard. He's got a lot to cram in since he's helping Uncle Steve so much."

"Yes, but…" Mrs. McCarthy leaned closer. "He's still interested in you, you know."

Ellie smiled. "I know. We're doing something tonight."

"Oh? What?"

"I don't know. Just that he said to dress warmly."

Mrs. McCarthy sighed. "Sounds romantic. I'm so glad for you both. You always seemed made for each other."

Ellie had to admit that she thought so, too. They were as good together as they had been in high school, only with some maturity behind them now. Enough to make grown-up decisions with wise hearts, not puppy love.

She took Mrs. McCarthy to the front for check-out, cleaned up her station, and welcomed her last client of the afternoon.

It really was a great day.

❄ ❄ ❄

THE CLOUDS CONTINUED through Saturday afternoon, promising snow soon. Wes put Sadie away quickly, fed the others, and gave Daisy her shot. Ellie filled his mind while he worked. How could he show her how much she meant to him? And how could they keep a long-distance relationship solid?

He wanted to bundle up and walk hand in hand with Ellie, with stars shining like a million crystal chandeliers above. He couldn't think of anything more romantic for her, but he'd have to settle for cold and cloudy through the town square tonight.

As he drove home, though, he passed Miraval, a fancy French restaurant. Maybe Ellie would like having an elegant evening away from all her worries. Just the two of them, talking and—he may as well admit it—gazing into each other's eyes.

Then he sighed. Miraval was undoubtedly expensive, and with the cost of college and vet school looming, he knew he shouldn't be spending money on anything but necessities. Besides, Ellie wasn't the type of gal to judge a guy by how expensive a date was. But how was he supposed to keep Ellie when he had absolutely nothing to offer? Not even a regular job, and his future would be a long time coming.

He trudged into Grandma's house, Kuda following close behind. He poured the Husky's kibble and microwaved a frozen burrito for himself.

Kuda gobbled his last morsel of food and nosed Wes for more. "Sorry boy. This is life for a while, boy. Better get used to it." Not that he would have gotten an extra treat anyway—Kuda was already gaining weight, just laying around these days.

Wes looked around as he ate. The house was coming along, despite the short amount of time he had to work on it. He still needed the realtor and the antique lady to come out, but most of Grandma's stuff was sorted, the clothes donated, and he was down to a single box of papers he wanted to keep.

He'd already fixed the kitchen, and the deck was looking

good. He supposed he'd spend the next hour before Ellie got off work getting the rooms ready to paint.

Wes had just pulled the last nail from the walls when his cell phone buzzed. He looked at caller ID in surprise for a moment, then clicked in to FaceTime. "Dad! How are you?"

His father was dressed in a t-shirt and shorts, two day's scruff on his face, and the sun ready to rise behind him. His rough voice sounded like he was just down the street, not across the world. "Doing fine, Wes, doing fine. Got up early but didn't have anything pressing, so I figured I might catch you."

Ten hours time difference, plus their work schedules, made phone calls rare. Wes grinned. "Good timing—I'm back in Huckleberry Falls for a bit, cleaning out Grandma's house —I think I texted you that. But I'm tired of all the nit-picky indoor jobs!"

Dad chuckled. "I'll bet. You're not happy away from the ranch, are you?"

"Actually…believe it or not, I'm thinking about college."

Dad raised his eyebrows. "Really? I thought you weren't that into school stuff."

Wes shrugged. "Not really, but I've realized I don't want to spend my life as a ranch hand. I guess it might be different if it were my own ranch, but that'll never happen. So," he took a deep breath, "I'm thinking about vet school."

His father's eyebrows lifted even farther. "You never even started college! So that's what, eight years of college?"

"I know. But Dr. Janssen pointed out that if I don't go to vet school, if I keep working at Black Rock, I'll still be thirty-eight by then. With not much to show for it."

Dad ran his hand through his close-cropped hair. "True."

As much as he liked the idea of becoming a vet, the conflicts of studying, finances, and Ellie still had to be worked out. But that wasn't anything he was ready to talk about yet. "What about you, Dad? Are you happy?" It was something he'd never thought to ask before.

"Me? Of course."

"No, really." For once, Wes wanted more than a quick, casual answer. "Do you like your life and where you are?"

His father thought a moment, then nodded. "I do. I'm only a roughneck, but I can troubleshoot with the best of them, and if I don't like one contract, there are a lot of other oil companies waiting to get me on their team. It's a nice feeling."

Wes was glad. It would be hard to think of his dad so far away and not liking what he was doing. His own situation kept popping to the front of his mind, though. "Uh, maybe I don't have the right to ask this, but are you dating? Do you miss being married?"

Dad threw his head back and laughed. "Oh boy, you know how to get to the point!"

"You don't have to answer if you don't want." Wes certainly wouldn't want to talk about his own relationships, but he needed to know about his dad.

"That's okay. Yes, I date sometimes, but nobody seriously. It's hard to work into an oil rig life. And as far as marriage is concerned, the best thing I've ever done was divorce Barbara. I can come and go as I like, I've got no one depending on me, no nagging, nobody wanting something I can't give."

"You sound like Jack and Johnny." Wes remembered a fishing trip as a teenager and the tales his dad's cousins had told.

His father laughed again. "Maybe it runs in the family. Maybe the Colton men aren't meant to be married." His face sobered. "Except for your mother. I wouldn't trade her for anything."

That left an awkward moment—the pain was always too heavy to talk much about Wes's mom. Finally, Wes asked what his father was doing for Christmas.

"In a mostly Muslim country? Not much. Probably just grilling with some of the guys."

Which wasn't much different than what Wes would be doing, except he'd be back on the ranch and indoors. Or here in Huckleberry, still indoors.

They talked a few minutes more, then said goodbye.

Wes went back to prepping the walls, thinking about how to fit a college schedule into his life. Thinking about the distance he'd be putting between him and Ellie, and wondering if he was one of those Colton men who wasn't meant to be married.

His ups and downs were like a rollercoaster he had no hope of smoothing out.

15

The clouds that had promised snow through the day finally delivered, and flakes fell lightly as Ellie touched up her makeup and gathered her pink scarf and mittens. Who cared if they clashed with her red hair—they made her happy.

Wes arrived, looking lean and sexy in his jeans and boots, although his big ranch coat hid his muscles. He reached forward for a quick kiss, but Ellie soon found herself melting against him, savoring every touch and tingle.

"That's quite a hello," she said when she could stand up again.

He leaned his forehead against hers, his arms loose around her back, and just stood there for a few minutes.

"Is something wrong?" This wasn't typical Wes behavior.

He shook his head. "Just enjoying the moment. You ready?"

She locked the door and slipped her hand into his arm. "Mm hmm. Mom's already got Olivia for the evening." A few steps took them around her apartment building, and then they were in the town square, snowflakes drifting slowly down around them.

Ellie sniffed at a sweet smell.

"Good idea," Wes said, following her gaze. He bought two hot chocolates from the sidewalk vendor, just before he closed up. Brushing a bench off, he motioned broadly. "A seat for you, madam?"

Ellie grinned and let him steady her onto the bench. He sat close, and they looked up and caught snowflakes on their tongues while their chocolate cooled.

Snuggles, sneaking glances, stealing a chocolatey-kiss or two…it was magical.

"Come on," Wes said, pulling her over to the carousel, its multitude of lights shimmering in the snow.

There were only a few people riding—most had gone home or back to their hotels to wait out the snow—but one set of parents were trying to comfort a screaming toddler.

"It's fun, see?" the dad encouraged. The child squirmed on the gaily-colored giraffe, reaching desperately for his mother.

"Uh, let's wait a bit," Wes said. He snugged Ellie under his arm and kissed the top of her knit cap.

When the distressed family finally gave up, leaving only a few people who were enjoying the ride, Wes pulled her aboard. "Would the lady prefer a horse or a circus animal?"

Ellie grinned. "Anything that goes up and down."

They picked a saddled zebra and a horse outfitted for royalty, and as the carousel started and the music played, they held hands, laughing as they moved up and down in opposite timing.

"I wish this had been here when we were kids," Wes said.

"That would have been fun. Oh, hey, Merry!" Ellie introduced her newly-arrived future business partner to Wes as they got off.

He tipped his cowboy hat to Merry. "I think we met at the Tree Festival. Or Festival of Trees. Whatever it was called, it's nice to see you again."

Merry smiled. "You, too. Having fun tonight?" Her eyes held a wicked gleam.

Ellie quenched the teasing with a glare. "We are. And where's …?"

"Carlisle? Probably on a ski slope up at Edelweiss. I had to work later than you, remember?"

"Right," Ellie grinned. "Some people just plan better than others."

Merry laughed. "And some people will have an incredible dinner at the Chalet at Edelweiss tonight! See you guys later."

Ellie watched her go. "It's fun to see people fall in love." She hoped Merry and Carlisle would make it long-term, but it reminded her that she had her own problems. She had fallen back in love with Wes, or she had never quit loving him, but she didn't know what their future would be.

"Yeah, but Carlisle? Who goes for a guy named *Carlisle*?"

Ellie looked up at him wryly. "Merry, evidently. And you can't judge someone by their name."

"I'll bet he's rich. And English or something."

"Well, yes. English *and* rich, actually. But he's a nice guy!"

Wes just shook his head. "Right. But I'm glad you like guys with normal names."

"Like Wes?" She laughed. He was so down-home, such a regular guy who still managed to find a few romantic gestures, she loved him even more. Sometime soon, though, she had to force the question: what were his plans now?

"Yes ma'am," he said, bringing her back to their comments about names. "Wes is a perfectly good name. Now, want to ride again?"

But the snow was falling harder and the carousel was

closing. Wes's mouth turned down. "Dang. I had hoped for at least three rounds."

Ellie kissed his chilled cheek and pulled him in for a hug. "It doesn't matter. This has been a wonderful evening." Snowflakes, hot chocolate, carousel rides—who could ask for more?

"Yeah, but I don't want it to end. Want to come to my place?"

Ellie gave him *the look*. The one she had perfected on both Olivia and Abby. The one that said, "Are you crazy?"

His hands raised in protest. "No, no, nothing like that! I was thinking a movie."

"Ah, in that case, definitely. Except...what about the snow?"

"We'll be fine. There's a reason I call my truck Old Faithful."

They kicked snow into the air on the way to the apartment parking lot, and the truck didn't slip once going to his grandmother's house.

❄ ❄ ❄

"Vet school?" Ellie asked, seeing the University of Wyoming printouts on Wes's table. "You're going to do it!"

"Maybe," Wes said, holding up two DVDs. "Action or comedy? I'm fresh out of romantic chick flicks."

Ellie looked at the two. "Comedy, please. I'm not into tension tonight. And why maybe?"

Wes let his breath out with a whoosh. "Because I don't know how to make it work. It's all so expensive. And intimidating."

The light, magical feeling of the evening suddenly became serious.

Ellie took the DVDs out of his hands. She grasped his arms and stared into his eyes, trying to make him believe what she already knew. "You can do this, Wes. It's intimidating because you don't know what to expect, but once you get started, you'll be okay. And there are scholarships out there—there's got to be something for you."

He looked away. "What if I can't do it?"

Ellie reached up and turned his face back to her. "Then at least you'll know you tried. Just like I'm trying with buying the salon."

"That's a huge commitment right there," he murmured, dipping his head.

She felt his breath on her face, saw his eyes soften. She stretched up to meet his lips, warm, soft, tender.

He groaned and clasped her head, pulling her closer, deepening the kiss. The feel of his fingers in her hair, of her hand on his clean-shaven cheeks, of her body molded to his… she wanted more. More kisses, more caresses, more *him*.

Ellie pulled back. They were approaching the point of no return, and someone had to keep a clear head. She filled her lungs with air and tried to calm her racing heart.

Wes swayed slightly, eyes closed. He opened them slowly. "I still love you, you know. I don't think I ever stopped."

She blinked. "Me too," she whispered. "My brain doesn't like it, but my heart remembers." She stepped back. "I think I'd better go."

Wes nodded, but reached the back of his fingers up to caress her cheek. "We can make this work."

Ellie caught her breath. Vet school in Laramie. Or out of state. "Can we?"

Because if they couldn't, her heart would splinter into icy shards.

She wriggled silently into her mittens and coat, pulled her

cap on, and wound her scarf around her neck. Down deep, she knew this thing between her and Wes was a sweet fantasy, a dream that wouldn't work in the light of day. She wasn't ready to wake up, though.

Forcing a light tone into her voice, she asked, "How about a ride home, Cowboy?"

16

"Dress warm again," Wes told Ellie on the phone Monday.

"Don't you have a house to work on?" Ellie's voice wasn't as upbeat as he was used to. Maybe spending Sunday away from each other hadn't been such a good thing.

"What's wrong? Don't you want to go out?"

"It's just...no, it's okay. What time?"

"As soon as you get off work. I'll do the horses quickly."

Ellie agreed, and Wes buzzed with excitement. This would surely bring back memories for Ellie, although unlike high school, he'd leave the trumpet at home.

He finished the sleigh rides by four-thirty on the shortest day of the year. Done with the horses by five-fifteen, even giving Daisy her last penicillin shot. Cleaned up, Chinese take-out in hand, and outside La Chevelure by six.

Ellie looked tired when she came out, and he wondered how she managed to be on her feet all day long. He worked hard, but a lot of it was sitting on a horse—or sleigh, right now—or *doing* something, not standing in one place. "Hi, Beautiful," he said, opening the truck door for her.

She accepted his hand to climb in and sighed in relief as she sank into the bench seat. "Smells good in here."

He came around to the driver's side. "Long day? People being difficult?"

"No more than normal." She leaned her head back and closed her eyes.

He'd love to take the pressure off her—it couldn't be easy being a single parent. But his plans were pressure in themselves. Still, he would support her however he could. He reached over and squeezed her hand.

She squeezed back lightly, but didn't open her eyes. "So where are we going?"

"You'll see." His buzz came back. He wanted to make her happy, lighten her load a little.

He took the highway toward the ski resort, then turned onto a small road. It had a few tight curves, and Ellie opened her eyes. "Wes, what are we—"

Her words cut off as he pulled into the overlook, a small parking area with a snow-covered picnic-table. "Remember this?" He came around the truck and opened her door. She took his hand to get down, but dropped it quickly and turned to face the road.

"What? Come on." He tugged her toward the view. The town lights sparkled below them, reflecting off the snow and making the valley glow. He could see the town square lit with Christmas sparkles, the movie theater, the dark ribbon of the river winding through. He didn't understand why she was so withdrawn. "Look, you can even see the Christmas tree and the carousel. And there's Steve's Trail's End Stables."

Ellie looked, but her expression belonged to a stranger. She wrapped her arms protectively around her body.

Wes ached to see her this way, here in their special place. Sure, this was where they had come to make out, but it was also their place to talk about serious things or to share some silliness that no one else would understand. "Ellie, I thought you would like this!"

She shook her head, her eyes welling with tears. She brushed them away angrily. "Sorry. I didn't mean to get emotional. But this is where we used to talk about hard things, and I'm afraid we're going to do the same now."

All of Wes's apprehension about his future, *their* future, returned. He'd put it out of his mind for a light-hearted date, and now it was right back in his lap. "I didn't want to do this now," he said. "I wanted tonight to be fun."

Ellie brushed the snow off one side of the picnic table. "We're adults now, Wes. We don't get to have fun all the time." She motioned to the other side. "Welcome to my parlor," she said with a sad smile.

Wes sighed, but cleared the rest of the picnic table and settled across from her. "Our pants are going to be wet," he warned, reaching across for her hands.

She just shrugged. "We've got some figuring out to do, don't we? We can't just stay in our fantasy world."

He froze inside just thinking about the words. "I know what I want—you *and* vet school—but I don't have a way to do it yet." How could he have the woman he loved when his future would take him away? But how could his future mean anything without the woman he loved?

"You know I'm buying La Chevelure. I'm meeting Alice again tomorrow."

"Which ties you firmly to Huckleberry Falls. Not to mention that your family is here." There was no way Wes would take her dream away, but no way for him to work with it.

She studied their linked hands. "And you're leaving." Her voice broke on the last word, but she plowed ahead. "Either for college or back to the ranch, but you're not staying here, are you?"

Despair pressed in. Wes pulled her mittens to his lips and kissed them.

She didn't look up.

"I don't even know how to afford college yet", he said. "But what about a long-distance relationship? If people love each other enough, they can make it work." Wes asked the question, but didn't really want to hear her answer. His brain already knew there was only one direction for them, had probably known it for a while, but he wanted to stay in denial a while longer. Like Ellie had said a few days ago, his heart couldn't bear admitting it.

Ellie looked up, looked past him. "You know that's not going to work for us. We need to be partners, leaning on each other. We've both got big challenges ahead of us. We need to be around to help each other, not making phone calls across the country." She paused for a long moment, then added, "And Olivia deserves a full-time father."

Olivia. Wes had fallen in love with that little girl, just as much as he had with her mother.

Ellie met his eyes now. "Do you know we sat right here, just like this, when you told me you wanted to see the world for a little while? That we could pick up again in a couple years?"

Wes clenched his jaw and fought to corral his emotions. "I thought this would be a happy place tonight."

It was Ellie's turn to squeeze his hands. "I think your subconscious knew, and knew it was time." She paused. "Olivia's going to miss you."

Wes groaned inwardly. "I'll miss her too. She's a sweetheart."

And what about you? He wanted to ask. *Will you miss me too?*

They stood, but after two steps toward the truck, Wes froze. No. He wasn't going to let this happen without fighting for what he wanted.

He pulled Ellie back to him. "Don't you care, Ellie? I feel like I'm breaking in pieces, and you're sad but very accepting of this. I thought you loved me!"

She stilled, resisting his pull. Her eyes turned from dull and sad to flashing angry. "You have no right to lecture me, Wes Colton. You're the one who kept us apart for nine years."

"I know, and I'm sorry, but that doesn't mean we can't make it right." He had to get her to reconsider.

Ellie crossed her arms, her body stiff, wisps of hair blowing in the wind. "I'm not a carefree teenager anymore, Wes. I'm not even a free-wheeling single. I'm a parent. I have a daughter to consider, to provide a stable home for. I have to protect her as much as myself."

"So that's what you're doing? Protecting yourself?" He couldn't help lashing out.

She turned her back on him again. "What if I am? You hurt me too much before, and now it's happening again. It's as much my fault as yours this time, I won't do a long-distance relationship. I won't do that to myself, and I won't do it to Olivia."

Wes clenched his jaw so hard he thought it would break. The lights from the valley weren't joyous anymore; their glare was sharp enough to cut him into slivers. His muscles trembled, their tension forming a straitjacket around him, keeping him from shattering into a million pieces.

Even to him, his voice sounded dead when he spoke

again. "I'm almost done with the house. I'll be gone right after Christmas. You won't have to worry about running into me." He hunched into his coat.

Ellie took a step sideways, away from him. It left him emptier than he'd ever thought possible.

"Let's go," Wes finally said. "Dragging this out won't make it any better."

She didn't meet his eyes as he helped her into the cab of the truck.

17

Wes forced himself to work the next morning, shoving any thoughts of Ellie into a tight box at the back of his mind, like a steer crammed into the chute for the vet.

He'd risen at five—hadn't slept much anyway—and put another skim coat on the drywall patches. Kuda ran in the snow while Wes loaded Sadie into the trailer. He had to grit his teeth through the sleigh rides; listening to happy Christmas conversations just didn't do anything for him today. He tuned out the voices he could and made plans: if he put his mind to it, he could finish the last repairs and get the painting done by the end of Christmas Day. He'd get the furniture picked up the morning after, and then hightail it out of town.

Wes groaned. Furniture. Antiques. Mrs. Abernathy had never come out, and he hadn't followed through. He'd spent too much time having fun with Ellie.

He pulled Sadie to a halt next to the Town Square, keeping his eyes away from Ellie's salon. Well, not hers yet, but if everything worked out for her the way she wanted, it really would be her salon. He wanted to be happy for her, trying to convince himself that if they couldn't be together, at least she'd have her business dream.

Words couldn't convince his aching heart, though. All the joy had gone out of the air, and nothing seemed to have much purpose.

He helped his passengers down from the sleigh, forcing a smile for the twin girls, and sighed in relief when there was no one waiting.

One foot in front of the other, he reminded himself. *A man can't do any more than that.*

The next plodding step was to call Mrs. Abernathy.

"I'm so sorry," she said when he greeted her over the phone. "I never made it out, did I?"

"No ma'am. But I'd sure appreciate it if you could squeeze me in tomorrow night."

"Oh dear. Tomorrow night is the Chamber Ball."

Right. The fancy Christmas dance he'd been planning on taking Ellie to. She wouldn't want to go with him now, but the thought of holding her in his arms on a dance floor squeezed the breath out of him.

"Would tonight work for you?" Mrs. Abernathy's voice came from far away.

"Tonight?" he stammered, trying to focus. "I suppose, sure. Eight o'clock?"

"I'll be there. I promise." The antique dealer said goodbye, and Wes sighed in relief. One more thing off his list.

He spent the afternoon with more sleigh rides, but he called it quits a little early. He hoped people hadn't minded that he wasn't in a jolly Christmas mood.

When the horses were taken care of, he knocked on the back door of the house and entered. Steve was grumbling at the TV in the dark.

Wes flipped the light switch on, but nothing happened.

"Couldn't stand on the blasted step stool to change the blasted bulb," Steve grumbled.

Wes changed the bulbs in the overhead light, then took a seat in the faded armchair across from Steve. "I need to talk to you."

"That doesn't sound good." Steve studied Wes's face. "It's not about the horses, is it?"

Wes shook his head. He stared at his hands. Took yet another deep breath. "I'm leaving. Going back to the ranch. The day after Christmas."

"Is this about Ellie?"

Wes was silent.

"You're going to regret it," the older man warned. He slapped his hand on the arm of the couch a few times. "You do know she's the best thing that ever happened to you, and you for her?"

Wes shrugged. Of course he knew it. Just like he knew he'd never love anyone else the same way. "No choice," he managed to get out before his throat dried up. He tried to put horses in his mind instead, and could speak again in a moment. "Can you get someone else for the evening chores?"

"Won't be easy," Steve said, frowning. "It was nice not to have to worry about them with you in charge. But never you mind, we'll make do."

"I'm sorry. And Christmas Eve will be the last of the sleigh rides, too."

Steve nodded. "You still going to be a vet?"

Wes shook his head. "I don't know. Can't seem to make anything work. College classes, money..." If none of his hopes were possible, what was the point of anything? He pushed to his feet, automatically dusting his hands on his pants. "The horses are doing fine; everyone's healed and healthy. I'll check in with you again on Christmas Eve."

Back at Grandma's house—he'd never call it home again —Wes fed Kuda but didn't bother with dinner for himself. His appetite was gone, and there was no food that could fill the emptiness inside.

He replaced a baseboard in the laundry room, fixed the hinge on the back screen door, and finished painting the back bedroom. The doorbell rang, and he let Mrs. Abernathy in. She browsed through the house, pulling the furniture out to look at the backs, turning knick-knacks over, making notes and taking pictures all the time. She spent a lot of time with Grandma's dresser and seemed to catch her breath at the ugly green lamp.

"All right," she said, back in the living room. "I won't know for sure until I check some things, but I'm pretty confident that the tall chest of drawers is an actual Shaker piece from the mid-1800s. It doesn't have any of the telltale marks of modern tools, and if I'm right, it could be worth a good deal. Your grandmother's bedstead is old, but I'll have to do some research to pin it down. The rest of it is mid-century modern—standard 1950s design, good quality but nothing remarkable."

"Okay." Wes waited for her to continue.

"You've got some collectibles here that might be worth something. I can put you in touch with a dealer if you like."

Wes frowned. "I won't have time. Could you take care of it? For a commission, of course."

"I'm sorry, I didn't realize you had a deadline." She jotted a note on her paper. "Of course I can do that. Now this lamp…"

Wes laughed. "Grandma loved it, but I call it the ugliest

lamp in the world. Don't worry about it—I'll just take it to the thrift store."

Mrs. Abernathy gasped. "Never! You can't... I'd like to take it with me for a consultation, if I may. I'll give you a receipt so we're all above board."

"A receipt?"

"There's a good chance it's an original Tiffany and worth a pretty penny. I'll need to make some phone calls, and it would help if I had the lamp with me to answer unexpected questions."

Wes looked back at the ugly lamp. Wasn't Tiffany stuff supposed to be really beautiful? "Sure, whatever you think best."

Mrs. Abernathy steadied herself and went on. "Your grandmother also had some nice silver pieces to go with her place settings. Do you want me to handle those, too?"

"Yes, ma'am. The more you can take off my hands, the better." He paused. 'The thing is, I need everything picked up the morning of the twenty-sixth."

Mrs. Abernathy looked at her notes. "I'll arrange that, even if I have to put my husband to work. And I should have an answer about the lamp by then."

Wes walked her to the door, then headed back to the masking tape. All the energy he'd used to work earlier had disappeared. He ended up slouched on the couch with Kuda, stroking his thick fur and pondering over antique prices. She hadn't mentioned anything in particular, but he knew a new bedroom set was a couple thousand dollars. Would an antique be worth that much? If they could all add up to a semester or two's tuition, that would be a big help.

And the lamp! He would have tossed it, but if it brought him a couple hundred, he wouldn't turn it down. Who knew Grandma had such expensive taste?

What he wouldn't give to talk to her now. To hear her laugh, talk to her about lost dreams, get a hug filled with more enduring love than he'd known since.

But she was gone, never to hug or advise again. Dad was across the world and was only inclined to short advice and no hugs anyway. And Ellie...

He recalled the warmth of her body against his, even through the thickness of their coats. Her crazy, contagious laugh. The way he felt complete with her. That while there might be wonderful possibilities ahead, he was enough right now.

Ellie...Ellie would have the advice he needed. As a teenager, her wise words had kept him out of more than a few scrapes, and now they had opened his eyes to a career he could only dream about.

That was the problem, though. Even if the antiques brought him six or eight thousand dollars, that was only a drop in the bucket toward the dream Ellie had awoken. Worse than that, her thoughts had matched his last night: there was really no way for them to make a relationship work.

Would he have fought to find a way if she had wanted to?

Maybe, but he knew there weren't any new ways around their roadblocks.

His father's words echoed in his mind now: *Maybe the Colton men aren't meant to be married.*

It looked like he was definitely a Colton man.

E llie twisted a lock of her client's thick, blonde hair and
pinned it up. She took a long breath to calm her tight
stomach, but had to admit some of the sourness she was
feeling was envy. Other than the first haircut that morning,
every client was getting her hair done for the Chamber Ball
tonight. Smooth up-dos, riots of long curls, or long and sleek
and shiny—Ellie usually loved the feeling of creating
something beautiful, but tonight she'd rather be going to the
ball herself. She now knew exactly how Cinderella felt, left
behind by gorgeously dressed stepsisters.

She'd seen Wes out the window a few times, dropping off
or picking up sleigh ride customers, but had pushed him
resolutely from her mind. She let thoughts of him in now and
wondered how long he'd keep going that day. The weather
forecast called for four to six inches of snow late that night,
and the low clouds were that particular shade of opaque gray
that promised to deliver. She hoped...

Ellie didn't know what she hoped. She knew what she
wished, of course. She wished Wes were staying; she wished he

had the guts to take a chance; she wished he had never taken off in the first place; and she doubly wished she could breathe without aching with love for him.

But those were wishes. Hope required the possibility of coming true, and no matter how much she wanted something, she couldn't change the course of events. They had made their decision. Made it together, no less!

She forced a smile back on her face and handed her client a mirror to check.

"This is beautiful, Ellie! Thank you so much."

And then there was only Merry Hurst left. Merry, who would be dressed for the ball in a gown fit for Hollywood, with Prince Charming on her arm.

Yeah, being Cinderella sucked.

Merry bounced in, her long, glossy brown hair swinging from side to side. She came to an abrupt halt. "You look glum, my friend."

Ellie shook her head and motioned Merry to the chair. "Just spending too much time in my head. Are you ready for tonight?"

Merry grinned. "Totally. And Mom created the *ultimate* ball gown for me!"

"Oh?" Ellie raised her eyebrows as she combed through her friend's hair.

Merry nodded. "Close fitting here," she motioned with her hands, "and a long, full skirt. Very elegant. And oh, the color!" She let out a sigh. "Deep wine, and shimmery…just magical."

Ellie only nodded as she worked some styling product into Merry's hair. She had an emerald green gown of her own that Wes would never see.

"You really are awfully quiet, Ell. Want to talk about it?"

Ellie shook her head, then answered anyway. "It's just…I

should be ecstatic. I sent my counter-offer for the salon this morning, and Alice accepted it an hour later."

Merry clapped her hands under the drape. "You got it! I'm so excited for you!"

"For *us*, you mean. We're in this together, remember?"

"Of course. I'm with you all the way. But it will be yours, just like you dreamed."

"Subject to an accountant's review of the business, of course." Ellie focused on crossing and pinning locks of Merry's hair into an intricate pattern across the top of her head.

Merry finally broke the silence. "So why aren't I hearing more about your plans? What else is going on?"

Ellie almost broke then. Almost cracked and shattered in pieces across the floor. She blinked rapidly and inserted a hair pin just so.

Merry caught her eyes in the mirror when she looked up. "Ellie? Spill."

Ellie paused. "You know Wes and I broke up? It was mutual. I swear it was. He's leaving, I'm staying, and I can't do a long-distance relationship."

"Ri-ight?" Merry dragged the word out.

"So why am I so empty inside? I should be all excited about the salon and Christmas, and all I want to do is curl up and cry."

Merry twisted around to look into Ellie's face. "Oh, sweetie, your head says it was best, but your heart doesn't agree. And it's your heart that's overriding everything else."

The hurt rose up from deep inside Ellie, threatening to spill over. Her breath hitched, but she managed not to sob. "I don't think I can keep going like this."

Merry squeezed her hand. "You're grieving, and believe me, grief takes its own time."

"I'm sorry. I didn't mean to compare—"

"That's okay. Ray's been gone a couple years, and while I'll never try to 'get over' him, my heart has let go and told me it's time to move on."

"Really?" Ellie sniffed. "Carlisle?"

Merry's soft smile disappeared. "I don't know. He has a lot going on in England."

A disheartened laugh escaped Ellie's throat. "That makes two of us, then. Why can't we fall in love with guys who want to stick around?"

They stayed wrapped in their own thoughts while Ellie put Merry's hair up. "There," Ellie said, handing her the mirror and turning the chair so Merry could see the back. "It's got enough pins in it that you'd need to do cartwheels for it to come down."

Merry admired it from several angles. "It's gorgeous, Ellie, thank you."

Ellie sprayed a light mist of maximum hold and whisked off the drape. "Off to the ball, and don't forget to have a fabulous time!"

Merry twirled impishly. "I will!"

She said goodbye with a light kiss, and Ellie headed to the back for the broom, muttering, "Yup. Cinderella, cleaning up while everyone else is off for an evening of romance."

She scolded herself mentally. If Olivia acted like this, she'd send her to her room for whining.

Ellie dumped the dust pan with a clang. *Quit moping. Life goes on.* And it would, eventually. The pain of Wes would dull a little, then recede bit by bit. She should know—she'd been through it before.

She pulled her shoulders back and deliberately set her mind down a different direction: come the end of January, La

Chevelure would be hers. Her very own hair salon, complete with stylists, a clientele and a silent partner for support.

Amongst the papers from Alice were copies of past orders for styling products and the most recent inventory. She'd also included a list of suppliers for the other merchandise the salon carried—soaps and lotions, jewelry, scarves.

With nearly the entire town at the Chamber Ball, she should have a quiet night with no phone calls—the perfect time to wrap the last presents, sing a few carols with Olivia before bed, and then organize herself and her plans.

Still, she couldn't help but stand mesmerized at the salon's front windows. Wes was unhitching Sadie from the sleigh and leading her back to the trailer. What would he be doing tonight?

Over and done with, time to move on, she reminded her heart.

19

W es stroked Ellie's hair as she tenderly kissed his face. Her moist lips against his cheek, the corner of his eye, the side of his neck. He wrapped his arms around her, wondering when her hair got so thick, as she gave a long lick across his chin.

Wes's eyes shot open as he bolted upright. "*Urgh*! Get off me, Kuda!"

The Husky nosed his underarm and whined before jumping off the bed.

Wes flopped back against his pillow, wishing he could go back to Ellie's kisses. Wishing he could go back in time a week, before he and Ellie put logic over feelings. His arms felt terribly empty right now.

Light penetrated Wes's eyelids, and he pushed himself out of bed. The sun shining off the thick quilt of snow made it bright as summer. He stumbled to the window. "The weatherman got it wrong this time, didn't he, Kuda?"

Instead of the four to six inches called for, the snow had to be ten, maybe twelve inches deep. It hit the middle of the hubcaps on his truck and sat in tall, slender pillows on the mailbox and tree branches. The beauty of the light and shadow took his breath away.

Reality brought it back again; he had a lot of shoveling to do. There was no point in taking a shower until he was done, but he sat at the living room window and nursed a cup of coffee for longer than he should have. He wondered if Ellie was working today or if she'd stay home and cuddle up with Olivia. He didn't know when the snow had intensified, but he hoped the people at that Christmas Ball had made it home okay.

When he finally went outside, the McCarthy grandkids were building a snowman next door. Kuda went to "help," and they threw snowballs for him while Wes got to work.

Two hours of mindless labor later, the sidewalk and driveway were clear, and the plows had come through. After an hour of playing with the kids, Kuda had spent the rest of the time lying on the porch watching his owner work.

Wes chuckled and rubbed the Husky's head before putting the shovel away. "Come on, boy, I've got to get a shower before the realtor comes." If the roads were clear, Bob Wilson would show up on time.

WES WATCHED as Bob examined the house again. "You've done a great job on it. You'll be finishing the trim around the back door today?"

"Yeah." He frowned. That wouldn't leave him anything to do on Christmas Day.

"And it will be empty by Saturday?"

"Furniture, donations and trash gone on Friday. I've got somebody coming in Saturday to do a final cleaning." Because Wes wasn't going to stick around any longer than necessary.

His enthusiasm for vet school had disappeared, and Black Rock Ranch was calling to him more and more. His aching heart longed for a home where he knew he fit in, where he could just be himself, keep his head down, and do his job.

He was good at it, he enjoyed it, and it didn't carry the uncertainty and pressure of a major life change. The fact that it didn't include Ellie…well, she had her life and he had his, right? Eventually he'd come to terms with it.

"Keep your head down, do your job" seemed like a good mantra for his life.

"Wes?" Bob interrupted his thoughts. "Come look at these comps."

They sat at Grandma's dining room table—no more memories to build there, either—and discussed comparable properties, sale prices, and what Wes could expect to get for the house. Bob explained that he would have it staged and get pictures taken on Monday. The listing should be up on Wednesday.

Wes nodded blankly and signed the agreement, cutting his ties to Huckleberry Falls. He wouldn't be back—too much chance of running into Ellie. He'd like to know how she did owning her own business, and he'd love to watch Olivia growing up, but there was no way he'd be able to handle seeing Ellie with someone else. She was a wonderful woman; it wouldn't be long before she moved on and fell in love with some guy. He could only pray it would be someone worthy of her.

The thoughts left him with a tight throat and muddled mind, and it was all he could do to walk the realtor to the door and nod goodbye. He turned back and buried his face in Kuda's fur.

. . .

Two hours later, Wes stepped back and admired his precision with the back door trim. Work was always good for pulling himself out of a funk. His mitered corners fit well, the trim was already primed, and all it needed was a coat of paint.

Mrs. McCarthy stepped onto the back porch, startling him. "Looks good," she said. "Your Grandma would be proud."

He tipped his hat to her. "Thanks. I hope so." He wished he had done some of this for her a few years ago.

"You've been working hard. I thought you might need some sustenance." Mrs. McCarthy handed him a plate covered with foil.

He peeked inside, mouth drooling. Iced Christmas cookies and a few slices of fruitcake. Unlike most people's, Mrs. M's fruitcake was sweet and light and absolutely delicious. "You're spoiling me."

"You're worth spoiling." She grinned. "And I have to get my spoiling in before Ellie takes over."

His moment of happiness vanished. "Uh…Ellie won't be taking over."

Mrs. McCarthy gasped. "But you two are made for each other. Always were. What happened?"

Wes shook his head. "It just won't work. She's anchored here, and I'm staying on the ranch. Or maybe going away to college." He didn't know why he added that last—college was out of the picture now.

"But if you love each other…" Mrs. M's face was troubled. "Can't you make it work?"

"Long-distance relationships have too many horror stories about them, and we don't want to go through that. And she wants an in-person dad for Olivia. So it's…" He shrugged, then inhaled deeply. "Mrs. Abernathy will be picking up some furniture and other stuff on Friday, and the thrift shop will be getting the rest. Then Bob Wilson and his crew will be in and out, and the house will go on the market Wednesday. You'll have new neighbors soon."

Mrs. McCarthy's lower lip quivered, but she stretched up to give him a hug. "I will miss you. More than you know."

Wes just squeezed her tighter.

She stepped back. "Now be honest, young man. If you're not with Ellie, what are you doing for Christmas?"

"Forgetting about it." The words were out of his mouth before he could think. But what else was he doing? He wasn't giving sleigh rides. The repairs were done. He wasn't in the mood to go to Christmas services at Grandma's church. Maybe he'd go out for Chinese for dinner.

"No, you are not. You're coming over. First thing in the morning, and you can watch the grandkids open their presents. Or if you want to sleep in, come when you're ready. Turkey and ham for Christmas dinner."

He began to stammer an excuse, but she overrode him. "There will be enough people to keep your mind off other things. And who knows? Santa might even leave something in a stocking for you." With that, she gave him another hug and moved carefully down the porch steps.

Bemused, he watched her go. She was right, though. Spending time with a crowded family would keep him occupied. Better than moping around all day.

❄ ❄ ❄

ELLIE SHOOK her head at the contents of Christmas stockings strewn across the floor. Candy wrappers, small toys, nuts, oranges. Olivia and Sarah were absorbed in plastering each other with Silly String, complements of Santa.

Ellie and Olivia, plus Abby and Sarah, had spent the night

at Mom's. There was no way this grandma was going to be deprived of watching her granddaughters wake up on Christmas morning! Ellie was glad, not just for family, but for the distraction.

"Come on, girls, let's clean up the trash so I can help Grandma and Aunt Abby with breakfast."

Ellie caught squiggles of Silly String in her hair instead. Laughing, she held her arms out wide and growled. "I. Am. The. Silly. Monster! I'm going to eat you up!" She chased after the girls, who squealed and dodged. "If you pick up a piece of trash, you're safe from me! For a minute, anyway."

She chased, the girls swooped and grabbed wrappers, and the room was, if not tidy, at least not trashy in less than five minutes.

"Just in time," Mom said, bringing in platters with eggs and bacon. Abby followed with biscuits and butter.

"Yum!" Olivia shouted.

Sarah wasn't so happy. "Can't we open presents and *then* eat?"

"Nope," Abby and Ellie said together. Ellie shepherded the girls to the table.

Mom smiled. "You used to say that, too."

"I know," Ellie said. "I hated that we had to wait."

"But now?"

"Now we love that they'll eat something to counteract all that sugar!" Abby grinned.

They joined hands and said grace, with a special thank you for family and the birth of Baby Jesus.

Ellie *was* thankful. She had so many good things in her life—Olivia, her mother, her sister, a salon that she almost owned in a beautiful mountain town.

She looked around the table. Everyone was healthy, her mom had a good job, and while Abby was still having a tough time, at least she was hanging in there. Ellie tried to help when she could, but Abby was determined to make it on her own. She was more likely to step in and protect Ellie than accept help herself. Even if Ellie's love life was in the dumps, everything else was good.

"Ellie? Are you in there?" Abby snapped her fingers.

Olivia giggled. Ellie had zoned out for a while. She winked at her daughter. "Yes, Sis?"

"Mom was asking what Wes was doing this morning. When do you think he'll get here?"

And just like that, Ellie's thankful mood vanished. "He won't. He's probably packing to leave town."

Her mother and sister gasped. "I'll kill him," Abby said. "You broke up?"

Ellie nodded. "But don't go blaming him. It was mutual."

"As if!" her sister exclaimed.

"It was. I got him thinking about college and vet school—I told you that. Well, the upshot is that he'll be gone for years, and I'm buying the salon, so I can't go with him, so what's the point?"

"And you didn't tell us?" her mother asked.

Ellie shrugged. "I didn't want to ruin your Christmas?" Tears leaked down her cheeks. She may as well be honest. "I just…there's a big gaping hole in my heart, and I didn't know how to talk about it."

Mom and Abby hurried to her, but before they could envelope her in a hug, Olivia spoke up, her eyes awash with tears. "So Mr. Wes isn't going to be my daddy like I was singing?"

Ellie's lower lip trembled as she shook her head. "No, sweetie, he's not. He never was." She gulped air. "Excuse me." She pushed back and headed for the back porch, grabbing her jacket on the way. She was not going to let herself break down in front of her daughter. She managed to keep the sobs at bay until the storm door closed behind her.

As empty as she'd been, she hadn't let herself cry it out. Not at work, not in front of Olivia, not at night by herself. With every day that passed, their logical decision seemed to bring more heartbreak, until she spent hours staring at the ceiling before she finally fell into a painful, restless sleep.

Now, in the frosty air, she leaned against the back of the house, shoulders heaving and tears streaming, a guttural sound coming from deep inside her. She barely heard the back door close again, but she felt the loving arms around her. She turned into Abby's embrace and sobbed.

Abby just held her, stroking her hair and murmuring soothing words, although Ellie couldn't say exactly what.

Long moments later, she pulled back. "Sorry, I couldn't keep it in anymore."

Abby gave a soft chuckle. "Maybe that's the problem. Maybe you need to let loose a little more."

"If I did, I'd probably never stop." Ellie smiled wanly. "It really doesn't make sense for Wes and me to be together, but my heart is just so empty. I love him more than ever, and it's not fair!"

"Oh, honey." Abby pulled her back into a hug. "Life isn't fair. Haven't you learned that by now?"

Ellie sniffled. "Yeah. Of course. But that doesn't stop me from wanting it."

"So what now?"

"Now I dry my eyes, put on a happy face, and go back in to our daughters. Maybe I'll see Wes in another ten years. He'll be a vet, and I'll be a busy shop owner, and it won't work all over again."

"Or you'll both forget each other and be married to someone else."

Ellie gave her sister a knowing look. "He might, but I won't marry again. And besides, you're a cynic."

Abby lifted one shoulder. "I've got good reason to be."

"True, that." Ellie gave her sister another hug. "And now let's go back to our kids. We've got Christmas presents to open, after all."

20

———

Wes pulled the pillow over his head and squashed it against his ear. Maybe if he ignored it, the phone would quit ringing.

It did.

He settled happily back into his dream of Ellie riding the open range with him.

The phone interrupted his dream again. Groaning, he reached out and answered.

"Merry Christmas, son!" His father's booming voice made Wes smile sleepily. He stretched and yawned before he managed a, "Hey, Dad."

"Aren't you up? Did I count the hours wrong?"

Wes peered at the tiny numbers at the top of the screen. "No, you're fine. I just slept in."

His dad chuckled. "I guess Christmas doesn't hold enough excitement to get you up at five a.m. anymore."

"Not for a few years now, unless I'm on the schedule to feed the stock." He ran a hand over his face. "Merry Christmas, Dad. How's your day been?"

"Full of sun and good food. Just been waiting until I could call you, but I guess I didn't wait long enough." Dad smiled, and they chatted about spending Christmas at the beach, Dad's friends from Australia, and Wes's sleigh rides. Then Dad said, "So, have you thought any more about vet school? Still want to do it?"

Wes sagged inside. "I've thought about it, but I don't think it's going to work. Nothing is going to work."

"Wes? What's going on?"

"Nothing more than you'd expect. Vet school is a crazy dream—too long, too expensive, too far away."

Concern filled his father's face. "Those are just logistical problems to be solved for a dream you've only just discovered. They're not the reason for that look on your face."

"Yeah, well…" How could Wes describe what had happened without taking hours for all the details? "Remember when you said that maybe Colton men weren't meant to be married? I think I'm following in your footsteps."

"What? You never even mentioned a girl."

Wes closed his eyes and leaned back. "Yeah, well, remember Ellie McKean?"

"Of course. You two were joined at the hip. Your grandmother thought you were made for each other."

"Did you?" Wes needed to know.

His father snorted. "I was too infatuated with Barbara to notice much of anything. I'm sorry."

"Yeah, well, Ellie's back in town, and we reconnected. Stronger than before. I thought we'd stay together this time, but it's not going to work."

"Because?"

Wes turned the phone, not wanting his dad to see the pain that must show through. "Because she's settled here, buying the salon she works at. And because I'd be away at college for at least eight years. So what's the point?"

"Son, you've been apart for what, nine years? And what was the point of that?"

Wes looked at his father again and sighed. "Not much. Which is why I doubt I'll ever get married."

"What, did you get kicked in the head and not tell me?" His dad ran his hand through his hair. Several times. "Do you love her?"

Wes's heart tightened, and his throat closed up even more. When his voice finally worked, he whispered, "More than I ever did before."

"Look, son. The worst thing I ever did was marry Barbara. You know that. But the best thing I ever did was marry your mother." He scratched his head again, the sunlight reflecting off the water behind him.

"I never had the deep connection with Barb as I did with your mom, and I'm not sure if Barbara ever really loved me. But if you love someone, if she's good and honest and true and she loves you as deeply as you love her, then you don't give that up for anything. Not ranch work, not vet school, not anything. And maybe you'll be lucky enough to have what me and your mom had."

Wow. Wes didn't think he'd ever heard his dad say so much about his relationships. Certainly not so passionately. "Love before all else, huh?"

"Only if it's right. And if it is, then everything else can be worked out."

Was that true? Was there really a way he and Ellie could be together? He didn't want to have his hopes dashed again, or to dash hers, but the possibility hovered in the air.

"I need to think about it," Wes finally said.

His dad nodded. "Pay attention to how you feel while you

think. Your mother would say to listen to God's whispers in your heart, and I never knew her to go wrong when she did that." He paused and looked away.

Wes's memories of his mom had never given him any guidance for adulthood, and he was blinking his own tears back now. What kind of advice would she give him now?

His father cleared his throat. "One more thing. If you think eight years for college is a long time, how does that compare with the rest of your life?" He paused, started to say something else, then stopped. "And that's enough serious stuff for one day, right?"

Wes grinned. That was the father he knew. "Right. Enjoy your time on the beach, Dad. I'm glad you called."

They exchanged Merry Christmases and hung up, and Wes threw the covers back. Kuda wanted to be fed.

THERE WASN'T MUCH ELSE to do on the house, but Wes needed something to keep his hands busy while his mind wrestled with the things his dad had said. And with what he'd almost said.

He wiped out cupboards with a wet rag and wondered if he really knew his dad. He'd always thought of him as a man who either couldn't commit, or who committed to the wrong things. But what if, since his mom had died, there hadn't been anything or anyone who'd grabbed his heart and soul? What if Colton men *were* meant to be married, but only to the right woman?

And what if Ellie was the right woman for him?

Wes shook his head. He already knew that. His whole being shouted for him to recognize that she was meant for him, that having her in his life was worth any sacrifice. She lifted him up, made him better than he could ever be on his own. She made him laugh, made him tender and soft-hearted, made him look for what could be, not just what was.

With her at his side, could he look ahead to something more in his life? Could she help him find a way to make it through vet school? And before that, help him through his undergrad? He might not manage it on his own, but he knew Ellie's support and confidence in him could carry him through anything.

He rinsed his rag and dried his hands, staring out the kitchen window to the snow-covered backyard.

Life with Ellie would be...ecstatic. No, it would be more than just superficial highs. It would be solid, caring, working together, and filled with a deeper love than he had ever known existed back in high school. Her flashing green eyes teasing a smile out of him. His hands through her hair. His fingers massaging her shoulders and feet after a long day at work. Her soft body next to his.

The backyard filled with imaginary children throwing snowballs, laughing and crying and coming in frozen for hot chocolate. His and Ellie's children, with Olivia taking charge of the little ones.

Wes's heart swelled at the thought. Ellie, the mother of his children.

He shook himself out of it.

How? How could they ever make this work? If he was to have Ellie in his life, if she'd even agree, he wasn't going to leave her and go away to college.

What did that mean? That he would pump gas or flip burgers just to be with her? What kind of a life would that be, for any of them?

He just couldn't see it. He wouldn't be happy, which would make her not happy. They'd get on each other's nerves and ruin everything.

Don't give up so easily. He looked up sharply, expecting to see Grandma standing behind him, but it was only her voice in his head.

She was right, though. If he let what-ifs keep him from Ellie, he wasn't worthy of her. If his heart was right, he could let possibilities bring them together instead of breaking them up.

His heart knew the truth—Ellie was worth everything he had to give.

Another thought came to mind, and he dropped the rag into the sink. He needed to spend some time on the computer.

Before he left the kitchen, he lifted his gaze to the ceiling. "Thanks, Grandma. I love you."

Two hours later, when one of Mrs. McCarthy's grandkids came to get him, he had to say no. "Tell her thank you, but I have something urgent to do. I'll tell her later, but she'll like it."

21

The text was short. Ellie didn't even have to unlock her screen for the words to take her breath away.

WILL YOU MEET ME AT THE BARN IN AN HOUR?

She had spent all of Christmas day focusing on the delight of the kids and the contentment of being with her family, managing to keep Wes tucked away in a corner of her mind.

With ten short words, he had her heart lifting and her stomach churning. What did he want? It had to be important to take her away from her family on Christmas, but hadn't they said everything there was to say?

He was leaving town tomorrow. Did he just want to say goodbye again?

She shouldn't even be considering it. Seeing him again would only deepen the wound, and it hadn't had time to grow even the slightest bit of scar tissue yet.

"Ellie? What is it?"

She gave a quick shake of her head. "Nothing, just thinking."

Abby frowned. "You've been staring at your phone for five minutes now. It's not nothing."

Ellie glanced at her sister, then looked out the window, wondering how to answer. A cardinal swooped and landed on a snow-covered branch, scarlet feathers fluffing against the frosty white.

She sighed and handed her phone to Abby, who read it quickly.

"What? You're not going, are you?"

In that instant, she knew. If it was one more goodbye kiss before she never saw him again, then so be it. She had plenty of nights ahead to cry. But if there was a chance that something might change, that she might be able to have this man she loved…

"Of course I'm going." Ellie shut her sister's protests down with a cool glare. "But first, Mom needs help with the pie."

She stood, only to notice Uncle Steve watching her instead of the football game. He winked. "Don't be late getting over there, now," he said.

She stared at him, but he just turned back to the game, a knowing smile on his face.

Ellie spent the next fifty minutes eating pie, playing Barbies with Olivia and Sarah, and catching glances from Uncle Steve. He refused to answer any questions, so in between conversations with Ken, Barbie and Skipper, her mind played with the possibilities.

What did Wes want? What could she expect from him? That he would give up vet school to stay with her? Hah! As if that would ever happen.

A little voice played in her mind. "Would you even let

him sacrifice that for you? What are you willing to give up for him?"

Just what was keeping her from going with him, anyway? La Chevelure, of course. Her dream.

But if the unexpected opportunity had never occurred, she would have dropped her job in an instant. It wouldn't be hard to find another salon to work in, no matter where his schooling took them.

So did she really have to stay committed to buying La Chevelure? Was she willing to give up her dream for his?

She envisioned owning the salon without Wes in her life, working long but fulfilling hours, raising Olivia on her own with her family close by. Her heart swelled with satisfaction, until she also envisioned giving up the salon to follow Wes. Eight years of supporting him through college, making a home that included both him and Olivia, laughing and loving together.

The heart that had swelled was now broken again at the thought of not having Wes. Why, oh why, couldn't she have both? Why should she have to choose? Why should either of them have to give up their dreams?

She wanted to shake her fist at life, but instead, she said goodbye to her mother and sister and put her coat on.

She hugged Olivia before going out the door—she didn't know what Wes had to tell her, but she was grateful she'd always have her daughter.

THE BARN LIGHTS shone brightly as Ellie pulled into the stable driveway, sparkles of light shimmering on the frosted snow.

Wes stepped out of the shadows, his heavy jacket

protecting him against the cold, his black Stetson tipped down so she couldn't see his eyes.

What did he want?

Her heart pounded, telling her exactly what *it* wanted.

Wes was opening her door before she had the parking brake on. He held his hand out to her.

"Wes, what's going on?"

"Shh, no questions." He held his hand out again, and this time she took it. He walked her down the side of the barn to where the light was on in the back. "Your carriage awaits, my lady." He swept his arm out expansively.

There behind the barn, in the lane that ran between the pastures and the woods, stood Sadie in full harness. She had silver tinsel braided into her mane to go with the jingle bells on her harness, and the red sleigh, polished to a shine, sat ready behind her.

Ellie turned to Wes. "But it's dark. You can't take her out in the dark!"

Wes just smiled, his twinkling eyes softening the hard planes of his face. He helped her up to the driver's bench, tucked a heavy blanket around her lap, and then climbed up beside her. "You'll see." He slapped the reins against Sadie's rump and they walked forward.

Ellie gasped as they left the glare of the overhead lamp. Small, twinkling lights were strung from tree to tree, followed by lanterns as far as she could see. "You did this?"

Wes nodded. He opened his mouth, but closed it again without letting words out. Another slap of the reins, and Sadie moved into an easy trot.

The magic of the night filled Ellie. The snow sparkled and glowed under the lanterns, Sadie's silver tinsel gleamed while her bells rang out, and the sleigh runners whooshed along beneath them. She laughed lightly and tucked her mittened hand under Wes's arm.

"You did this. For me," she whispered.

Wes looked at her now, a smile playing across his face. "Of course."

She hugged his arm and leaned against him as he drove. His powerful gesture was filled with enchantment, and she loved him all the more for it, but why? Had he changed his mind? Or was he trying to get her to change hers?

What would she say to either?

Ellie shoved the thoughts out of her head and focused on the night around them. The lights of Huckleberry Falls glowed a few miles away, but not enough to dim the stars above them. The moon snuck in and out of passing clouds, brightening the snowy field before leaving it in semi-darkness again. And always, Wes's warmth was beside her.

The lanterns finally ended, and Wes pulled Sadie to a walk. He guided her through a turn, but stopped when they were facing back to the barn. "Ellie, I've been thinking."

His eyes were warm and loving, but she saw concern in them too. She tensed involuntarily—which direction was he going to go, and how would she respond? "Wes, I—"

He put a gloved finger over her lips. "No, this is hard enough; let me say my piece. And then you can think about it —you don't have to give me an answer tonight."

Ellie took his hand away and gripped it tightly. "I'll listen."

W es reached up with his other hand and stroked her cheek lightly. Would she listen to all he had to say?

"I love you, Ellie," he murmured. "I always have and I always will. There won't ever be anyone else."

"I know, and I love you too, but we decided—"

"Nope, my turn." He looked forward to Sadie, then back to her, his heart full to bursting. "It's not just that there will never be anyone else. There isn't any*thing* else, either. Whether I try to be a vet or end up back on a ranch, nothing is worth it without you in my life. You are what I want most."

Ellie's eyes filled with tears, and he wiped one softly away. All the perfect words he'd practiced vanished, and all he had was raw emotion. He took both her hands in his.

"Ellie, I love you so much. I wish I had everything in the world to offer you, but if I can only see how to make things work for the next couple years, is that enough for me to ask you to marry me? Would you have that much faith in me?"

"Oh Wes, of course I would. But—"

He didn't want to hear her reasons why not. He put his

finger back over her lips. "No buts, not yet. I have to tell you what I worked out first.

"I want to be here with you and Olivia, but I need to go back to the ranch to tie things up. Then I'll use the next six months to study and remember all the things I've forgotten, and then I can take classes online for pretty much the first two years. I don't know how to work it after that, but—"

Ellie's kiss cut off his words suddenly. Not a gentle, tentative kiss, but firm and demanding. He let her claim him, wiping out all his words of reason and filling him with emotion and wonder instead. Her touch, her taste, her perfume filled his senses. She had one hand on his face and the other behind his head, holding him as if never to let him go.

He deepened the kiss, both hands in her hair now, and the world fell away for a few long moments. Wes finally pulled back to kiss the corner of her mouth, her nose, her eyelids. The precious spot right below her ear, then down her neck. He could feel her pulse pounding.

Wes closed his eyes again and took a long, slow breath. "I'll take that as a yes."

"A yes to what?"

He opened his eyes to see the corners of her mouth quirking up. "A yes to marrying me, of course."

Her mouth twitched. "But you haven't asked me."

"I did! I just—"

She grinned widely and shook her head. "You asked me if it was *enough* for you to ask me."

Oops. Trust Ellie to catch him out on his wording.

He sighed dramatically, pulled his hands away, and got out of the carriage. He knelt in the cold snow. Sadie turned her head to watch the silly human.

"Ellie McKean, I love you. I've loved you since I was

fourteen, and I'll love you forever. I promise to give my life for you, to protect you, provide for you as best I can, and to always be true. Will you do me the honor of becoming my wife?"

Ellie's laughing eyes turned serious. She stepped down from the sleigh and cupped Wes's chin. "Wes Colton, whatever you've planned for the next couple years, and whatever comes after that, I will also give my life for you, protect you, help provide for our family together, and always, always be true. I would love to be your wife." Then she grinned and pulled him to his feet. "Is next week too soon?"

"Yeah, probably," Wes said. "Your family might have something to say about that." He lost himself for an eternity in her eyes. "But we can certainly fill the time with more of this." He dipped his head and softly kissed her again. And again.

Sadie snorted and tossed her head, setting her bells to jingling.

E llie slept late the next morning—not surprising since she'd been too excited to fall asleep until four in the morning. She woke to Olivia's quiet conversations between Barbie and Ken at their new mansion.

"Hey, sweetie," Ellie said, tightening her fuzzy bathrobe around her. "Are you having fun?"

Olivia looked up with a joyful face. "This is the most scrumptious present *ever!*"

For a six-year-old, maybe. But Ellie could think of another, more scrumptious present—one wrapped in jeans and boots and hope. She crouched next to her daughter. "Want to go see Mr. Wes this morning?"

Olivia's face fell. "But he's not going to be my daddy."

Ellie planted a kiss on her forehead. "I think you'll like going over there."

Olivia shrugged and turned back to the dolls.

"Come on. We'll get dressed and make some lunch to take him."

Olivia sighed heavily and dragged herself to her room.

. . .

BY THE TIME they got to Wes's house, Olivia was almost as cheerful as Ellie, who marveled at her daughter's mercurial moods. Kuda greeted them on the driveway, and Ellie could hear the rhythmic *thunk* of someone chopping wood in the back. "Maybe Mr. Wes will let you build a snowman while he works," she said.

Olivia grabbed her hand and pulled her toward the sound.

Ellie stopped when Wes came into view. She watched the muscles ripple across his back, only the work and a flannel shirt to keep him warm. He was smooth and steady, focused on the task at hand. She hesitated to interrupt him, but the need to see his face was too strong to resist.

"Wes?"

He pulled the axe back mid-stroke, turned and dropped it. "Ellie!"

In three seconds, he had her in his arms, lifted high and twirling around.

She laughed, joy bubbling up and spilling over, drowning all the weight and worry she'd carried for so long.

He put her down then and kissed her. Tender, passionate, needy, giving—his kisses covered the whole range until she put her hands on his cheeks and held him still.

She touched his lips lightly with hers, their breath mingling, and gazed into his chocolate eyes. "I love you," she whispered.

"I love you too," he whispered back, eyes sparkling. "Want to go look at rings today?"

"Mommy?" came Olivia's puzzled voice.

Before Ellie could speak, Wes had turned to her and dropped to one knee.

Olivia giggled. "You're in the snow, Mr. Wes."

"I know, but I have a very important question for you, Oli—"

"Mr. Colton? Are you back there?"

Ellie gave Wes a questioning look.

He sighed and stood. "I'm here, Mrs. Abernathy," he called back. "Don't tromp through the snow—I'll meet you at the front door."

The three of them left their boots in the mudroom, and Wes let Mrs. Abernathy into the house.

"How are you, Mr. Colton?" she asked, removing her coat and gloves in the living room.

"Fine, thanks. But there's been a change of plans. We need to hold off on you taking the furniture." He put his arm around Ellie and grinned.

Mrs. Abernathy's eyes sparkled. "Congratulations are in order, I gather."

Wes nodded. "We won't be keeping everything, but we haven't decided yet."

"And the smaller items?"

Wes looked at Ellie. She smiled up at him and shrugged. She wasn't sure what his grandmother had, let alone what she —or Wes—would want to keep. "Do you like Hummel figurines?" he asked. "Or sterling silver?"

What could she say? She had no idea. She just knew she wanted to keep him.

He turned back to Mrs. Abernathy. "We'll have to let you know. But I know I don't want to keep the ugly lamp or the paintings."

Mrs. Abernathy cleared her throat. "About that lamp…it *is* a Tiffany, a design called Acorn, and it could be worth twenty-five to thirty thousand dollars."

Ellie gasped, and Wes almost missed the couch when he sat. "Tw-twenty-five thousand?" he croaked.

"Minus commission, of course." Mrs. Abernathy smiled. "Between the lamp and the furniture, I think you should clear about thirty thousand. Which would make a mighty fancy wedding."

Ellie goggled. No way would she want to spend that much on a wedding! She couldn't help but think that thirty thousand dollars would pay a lot of tuition. He could…They could…It was too much to think about. She lowered herself onto the couch next to Wes and sunk her head into her hands.

She felt Olivia's small hand in hers. "It's okay, Mommy. I love you." She rested her head against Ellie's arm. "I think Mr. Wes loves you too."

Ellie picked her head up to look at her daughter. "You know the best things to say, sweetie." She kissed her hair, then snuggled into Wes's arm.

"You're staying in the house? That takes the big rush away, doesn't it?" Mrs. Abernathy said. "I'll call you next week."

"Big rush? I have to call Bob!" Wes said, jumping up. He escorted Mrs. Abernathy to the door, then pulled out his phone.

Ellie put her hand on his. "There's no big hurry. No real estate stuff is happening this instant. We have time to talk about everything."

Wes sat back on the couch. "Thirty thousand dollars— that changes everything!"

"Ye-es," Ellie said. "But maybe you don't want to spend it on tuition right now. Maybe we should get through your undergrad and save the lamp for vet school. Or we could—"

Wes pulled her down and silenced her with a kiss. A kiss

she melted into, a kiss she savored and then owned, demanding more from him.

When they broke apart, Wes leaned his forehead against hers. "We've got plenty of time. No decisions now," he murmured.

Time, Ellie thought. All the time in the world, now that Wes was hers. Time to figure things out, but more importantly, time to love each other, to forget the past and make new memories. Time to grow old together.

"You're sure kissing a lot," Olivia piped up. "Does that mean Mr. Wes is going to be my daddy after all?"

Blood rushed to Ellie's face. She'd been making out in front of her six-year-old daughter!

"Olivia," Wes began, "I still haven't asked you that important question." He rose and took her hands, then knelt again—this time on worn carpet instead of wet snow.

"Miss Olivia McKean," he said solemnly, "I love your mother, and I love you. I will forever and ever. As her daughter, will you give your permission for me to marry her? And will you do me the honor of becoming my daughter, too?"

Wide-eyed, Olivia nodded. "You really will be my daddy?" she whispered.

Wes nodded in return, then kissed her on both cheeks. "I would love to be your daddy."

Olivia flung her arms around his neck. "I love you, Mr. Wes."

Ellie pressed her hand harder over her lips, but couldn't stop the tears streaming down her cheeks.

Wes Colton, former wanderer, future vet, fabulous father. Her cowboy.

EPILOGUE

Late May

"Wes Colton! Get out here!" Abby couldn't see him, but she knew her voice carried to the back of the barn.

Wes poked his head out of a stall. "Yeah?"

She stalked over to him, glad she hadn't changed her clothes yet. "It's your wedding day, doofus. What are you doing here?"

"Doctoring Beau's leg," he said, pulling out his phone. He yelped when he saw the time. "I was only supposed to be here a few minutes. Can you take this stuff to the tack room?" He held out a bucket filled with cotton, wrapping, scissors and a tube of medicine.

She took it gingerly, holding it far out to the side. "And that would be where?"

He pointed to the other aisle. "See the blue door? Just set it inside." He turned back to the horse.

By the time she reached the tack room, her almost-brother-in-law was running desperately toward the main entrance.

An hour later, Abby took one twirl for herself—the pale aqua gown made her look amazing—before she helped Olivia and Sarah into their pint-sized versions.

"This dress is magnificent!" Olivia exclaimed, fluffing the skirt. She danced around. "You look magnificent too, Aunt Abby. This whole day is magnificent!"

Abby grinned. "So that's your new word, huh? Here, Sarah, let me tie your bow so it will be *magnificent*."

When the girls were ready, she herded them down the hall to the large room where Ellie and Mom were. The make-up lady had just left, and Ellie looked beautiful even in her slip.

"Oh good, you're here," Mom said. "Are you ready, Ellie?"

Ellie nodded slowly.

Abby took her hands and looked into her troubled eyes. "It's okay to be nervous."

"Am I doing the right thing?"

Abby nodded, then pulled her sister into a hug, careful not to mess with her hair. "I've gotten to know Wes pretty well in the last five months. He's worthy of you."

Actually, Wes had shown himself to not only be a man of his word, but a man who loved Ellie deeply, putting her needs above everything else. Abby was ecstatic for her sister, but the old ache inside her reared up, reminding her that she didn't have anyone like that. And the chances of finding someone who fit her as well as Wes fit Ellie…well, Abby had made it on her own this far, she could make it through the rest of her life.

She stepped out of the hug and looked Ellie in the eyes. "You two are made for each other. You're both strong and supportive and deeply in love. You'll make it."

Ellie nodded, her eyes filling with tears.

"Oh, don't do that," Abby scolded lightly. "You'll smear your mascara. Let's get you into that gorgeous dress and out there to see your groom."

THE CHAMONIX HALL at the Edelweiss Resort had been transformed into a vision of springtime—peach-colored tulips mixed with aqua calla lilies and white roses. Tiny white lights twinkled through the peach and aqua tulle draped around the room.

Guests filled the white chairs, the minister stood under the bridal arch, and music rang through the air.

And Wes...Wes stood at the front, with a couple of cowboy friends as his groomsmen. He looked almost as nervous as Ellie. Abby gave him a wink, and he returned a weak smile.

At a nod from the minister, Abby nudged Sarah and Olivia down the aisle to scatter their rose petals. Merry Hurst, in a slightly darker aqua, went next.

Abby looked back at Ellie and Uncle Steve, blew her sister a kiss, then took her own measured steps down the short aisle.

She heard the subdued *oohs* from the guests when Uncle Steve and Ellie stepped into sight. Reaching the front, Abby turned to see Ellie's face glowing as her gaze locked onto Wes.

The bridal couple lit a candle together, exchanged vows, and shared a kiss that made Abby's heart melt. These two would be together for a long, long time.

The joy stayed with Abby as she walked back down the

aisle with Adam Black, Wes's old boss from the ranch. It stayed with her through the toasts at the reception. And it stayed through her first dance—with Adam, of course.

But as she ate the delicious treats and danced with random guys, one phrase started repeating through Abby's mind: *always the bridesmaid, never the bride.* It was nonsense, of course—this was the first time she'd been a bridesmaid, and she had already been a bride.

But to have the chance to be one again...she looked around the room. Adam was engaged, the two guys over there were married, those three drank too much, these three had been in high school with her (besides, *no way!*), this one was always gone on business.

That was the problem with living in a small town—she already knew everyone's flaws. She knew who played around, who was a chronic liar, who was a superficial as the polish on his car.

She sighed and went for another glass of punch, checking to make sure the girls were doing fine with her mother. As she reached for the ladle, someone else reached at the same time.

"I'm sorry, go ahead," a deep voice said.

Abby looked up into blue eyes she had never met before, to a smile she'd never seen before.

"H-hi," she stammered.

He smiled wider. "I'm Mark. I came over from Laramie to be my cousin's plus-one."

Abby found her voice. "I'm Abby. I'm the bride's sister."

Mark took the ladle from her hand and filled her cup. "Nice to meet you, Abby." He handed her the cup. "When you're done with that, would you like to dance?"

Abby looked over to where Ellie and Wes were dancing, totally entranced with each other, zoning out from the other hundred people. She looked over to Sarah and Olivia, sitting on either side of their grandmother. She looked back at Mark.

"Sure. I'd like that."

And she smiled.

THANK YOU

Thank you for reading *Sleigh Ride with the Cowboy*. I hope you enjoyed reading it as much as I enjoyed writing it!

Please consider leaving a review for it on Amazon or Goodreads. Authors love hearing from their fans, and word-of-mouth recommendations help other readers find books they'll enjoy. Thank you for taking the time to share your thoughts!

To find out about new releases, sales and give aways, sign up for Jen's sort-of-weekly newsletter.

(I don't spam and I don't share your email without permission.)

HUCKLEBERRY FALLS HOLIDAY ROMANCES

What happens when five clean romance authors start tossing ideas around? You get a whole new series!

Huckleberry Falls is a delightful fictional town in Wyoming, full of quaint and quirky shops, mountain skiing, and *loads* of holiday celebrations. And, of course, love is always in the air!

Huckleberry Falls Christmas 2020:

Merry and the Gentleman by Donna K. Weaver
Sleigh Ride with the Cowboy by Jen Peters
12 Days of Christmas Chaos by Wendy Knight
Deck the Halls by Leah Sanders
Pinecones and Huckleberries by Emily Dashmore

MORE BY JEN PETERS

The McCormick's Creek Sweet Romance Series

Trusting His Heart (#1, Cat & Justin)

Finding Her Heart (#2, Ree & Mitch)

Safe in His Heart (#3, Robin & Cliff)

Stealing His Heart (#4, Raine & Brandt)

The Christmas Key to Her Heart (#5, Nora & Forrest)

Protecting Her Heart (#6, Javi & Shauna)

Coming in 2021:

Brothers of Black Rock Ranch

(a Christian Cowboy Romance series)

ABOUT THE AUTHOR

Jen Peters loves being in love—the look in his eyes that makes her feel pretty, the whispers on the phone at night, the gentleness of his kiss, the security in his arms. She was lucky enough to marry her sweetheart all those years ago, and he continues to sweep her off her feet.

Whether reading or writing, Jen loves escaping into a romantic story to experience it all over again, especially when remodeling their homes gets a little overwhelming. Originally from Oregon, she and her family now live in central Indiana, where an opinionated Cavalier named Bailey reminds her not to take life too seriously.

Learn more about Jen Peters by visiting
www.jenpetersauthor.com

Follow Jen on:
Facebook
BookBub
Amazon